crackback

John Coy

Scholastic Press New York

LIBRARY OF CONGRESS CATALOGING-IN-PUBLICATION DATA

Coy, John. 1958-

Crackback / John Coy. — 1st ed. p. cm.

Summary: Miles barely recalls when football was fun after being singled out by
a new coach, constantly criticized by his father, and pressured by his best
friend to take performance-enhancing drugs.

ISBN 0-439-69733-6

[1. Football — Fiction. 2. Fathers and sons — Fiction.
3. Coaching (Athletics) — Fiction. 4. Steroids — Fiction.
5. Drug abuse — Fiction. 6. Schools — Fiction. 7. High schools — Fiction.]
I. Title. PZ7.C839455Cra 2005 [Fic] — dc22 2004030972

10 9 8 7 6 5 4 3 2 1   05 06 07 08 09

Printed in the United States of America   23

First edition, November 2005

Text type was set in ChiantiBT.
Display type was set in AdLibBT.
Book design by Marijka Kostiw

for the love

■ ■ ■ "Thumbs in. Grab and go!" Coach Stahl hollers as we line up for pass patterns. Ninety-five and humid and we've been practicing for three hours. I'm shot, but Coach keeps saying hard work in summer makes champions in fall. Over by the track, two linemen are down on all fours puking.

I run twelve yards, plant my right foot, and cut left. Jonesy fires a rocket. Instinctively I stretch my hands, little fingers together — the way Dad drilled into me in the backyard — and make the catch.

"Thumbs in, Manning." Stahl throws down his cap. "Can't you hear?" He holds his hands, thumbs touching. "Do it again."

I run my pattern and twist my arms around to make the catch.

"Grab and go," Stahl yells. "Don't do it half-assed."

I run hard upfield. I like Dad's way of catching better.

Zach Turner, my best friend, who starts at the other corner, runs his pattern. We both wear the dark blue jerseys of starters. The other guys wear white.

"That's the way, Zach." Stahl claps. Stahl teaches

gym. He's short, but he's got the big chest of a weight lifter.

Why's he insisting we catch like this? Dad always says fingers together is the natural way, like holding a watermelon.

When Stahl walks over to Coach Sepolski, the head coach, I put my hands out, fingers touching. It *is* more natural. On my next down and in, I catch that way.

"I saw that, Manning." Stahl rushes over. "If I say thumbs in, I mean thumbs in. You understand?"

"But Coach —"

Stahl grabs my face mask. "I don't want any of your 'but Coach' BS. You think you're so smart. Take a lap."

The other guys grin, glad it's me who's getting it from Stahl, not them. Everybody's sick of practice and ready for our first game tomorrow.

My Nikes kick up dust on the path around the fence. Stahl can be such a jerk. I was just experimenting.

"Head up. Dig! Dig! Drive your block," Coach Norlander calls. He's a big guy, but he's got a high voice. Linemen are cracking pads in a two-on-two hamburger drill near the fence. Tyson Ruden, our three-hundred-pound All-State tackle, runs over a sophomore like a semi crushing a cardboard box.

On the sideline, Sam Hunter and a group of second

stringers take a water break. Sam staggers around like a drunk, and guys laugh. He's not serious about football. Why isn't Stahl yelling at him?

A light breeze blows as I circle the backstop. This morning, Coach Sepolski asked us to set goals. I want to repeat as conference champs and go to the play-offs. I want to be named first team All-Conference and to one of the All-State teams. I want to win State. I want to show Dad how good I am.

On the tennis courts, the girls' team is hitting over-heads. They're wearing short shorts and sleeveless tops. I slow down for a look. This year, though, I'd like to do more than look. That's another goal. Megan Harkin hammers a smash so hard the ball sticks in the fence.

I turn the last corner and sprint back. "I've been coaching twenty-seven years, and I've had some excellent teams. This one has the potential to be the best." Coach Sepolski chops the air with his right hand. "Live up to that potential. Be the best football player you can be." He pauses to let it sink in. "Shower up."

"Manning," Coach Sepolski calls. "That's a bad way to end practice." He puts his hand on my shoulder, and I smell his Marlboro breath. "You're a junior now; I expect some leadership out of you. Listen to Coach Stahl. Is that clear?"

"Yes, Coach." Sepolski was my freshman biology teacher, and last year he picked me to start. Not many sophomores play varsity at Confluence, and at five foot eleven and 155 pounds I'm not that big. But I love to smash guys. Sepolski likes hitters.

"One more thing, Manning."

"Yes, Coach."

"Carry the tackling dummies back to the shed."

"Yes, Coach." Sepolski won't hold the lap against me. I'm afraid that Stahl will.

chapter two

❚❚ ❚❚ ❚❚ "C'mon, Man. Let's go." Zach's buttoning his shirt in front of the mirror. He fixes his collar and shakes his head to the music that's thumping through the speakers.

"I had to make a dummy run."

"You shouldn't mess with Coach Stahl."

"I wasn't messing with him, just practicing different ways to catch." I unsnap my shoulder pads and throw them into my locker. I peel off my T-shirt: FOOTBALL IS LIFE. EVERYTHING ELSE IS PRACTICE.

"Hurry up." Zach gels his hair. "I'll wait for you in the truck."

"Grab and go, grab and go." Jonesy's coming out of the shower. He's got a new tattoo on his shoulder, an eagle with outstretched talons. "Coach giving you dating advice? He knows you need help with girls. Unless you're sticking with boys."

"Shut up, Superstar." I snap my towel at him.

"Don't be playing with yourself." Jonesy snaps back. "You need to be at full strength tomorrow."

Tyson Ruden and some of the linemen are showering.

Tyson's arms are larger than my legs. He's huge everywhere. I wish I was bigger.

On the ride home, I inhale the AC. "I'm going to beat you on interceptions this year. I can feel it."

"You're on for a hundred," Zach says.

"A hundred? You want to bet a hundred bucks?"

"Can't handle it?" Zach shrugs his shoulders.

"I can handle it. You want to lose that much?"

"I won't lose." Zach stops for a red light.

"I won't either." We shake hands.

We drive down the hill into the valley where the Clearwater and Hahawakpa rivers come together. We pass Division Street, where Dad has his paint store. He should be home by now. No telling what mood he'll be in.

"What's your max on bench?" Zach asks.

"About 160." I can't exaggerate or Zach'll make me prove it. He weighs fifteen pounds more and has always been stronger.

"You should be lifting more."

"What're you doing?"

"Up to 220. I want to do 250." Zach pulls onto my street. "Got something for you." He grabs his gym bag, opens a bottle, and shakes out two gold capsules.

"What's this?"

"A little Rip Blast. Helps psych you up before the game."

"What's in it?"

"A jolt of caffeine. Like drinking a bunch of Red Bull, but you don't have to piss."

"I don't know, Zach."

"Tyson's taking 'em. Lots of the seniors. Gives you that edge."

I stare at the capsules. I've never taken anything for an edge. I get out and shove them in my pocket.

"Take the Blast before the game," Zach says. "Be ready to kill 'em."

"I'll be ready." I slap my hand on the door.

❚❚ ❚❚ ❚❚ The smell of garlic hits me when I walk in. "Those floors are clean," Mom says. "Take your shoes off."

"They're not dirty."

"Take them off, Miles."

In the living room, my eight-year-old sister, Martha, sings to *The Lion King*. "Oh, I just can't waaaaaaaaaaaait to be king!"

"Mom, I'm starving. When do we eat?" I kick off my shoes.

"Five minutes. Your father is cleaning up. Wash your hands and pour water."

"Why can't Martha do it?"

"She's busy."

"With what?"

"I asked *you*, Miles," Mom says.

I put ice in each glass and pour water from the blue pitcher.

"Martha, wash your hands." Mom brings in chicken, rice, and zucchini stir-fry. "Sit down, everybody, before the food gets cold."

Martha hurries to the sink. Dad clumps down the stairs. We all take our chairs on separate sides of the table.

"Let's pray," Mom says.

I bow my head and Dad leads the prayer.

"BlessusOLordandthesethygiftswhichweareaboutto receivefromthybountythroughChristOurLord."

"Amen." Mom passes the food.

"I heard something at the store." Dad scowls. He's got a deeply lined face and a scar on his cheek.

"What?" Mom pushes up her glasses.

"Someone was running laps at the end of practice." Dad glares at me. "Who was it?"

How does Dad know everything? "It was me."

"Why were you running?"

"Coach Stahl said I wasn't catching the ball right."

"I don't want to hear about you running laps."

"But Dad —"

"Listen." He cuts me off. "Listen to me. Listen to your mother. Listen to Coach Stahl. You haven't been listening lately. I don't want to hear that my son is running laps. Is that clear?"

"Yeah." I drop my head and pick at a piece of zucchini. He's the one who doesn't listen.

"You need to respect your coaches, respect your teachers, respect your parents." Dad grabs the shaker and salts his chicken.

Nobody says anything, so the only sounds are silverware clinking and people chewing.

What does catching a football have to do with respect? What about me? Is Dad respecting me?

Mom tries to change the mood. "Martha, how was Kelsey's house?"

"Fantastic. Kelsey's got a new ant farm. It's fun to watch them work. Ants carry loads that are much bigger than their bodies. People can't do that. That's why I think ants are stronger than people."

I'm relieved someone else is talking. Dad and I sit on opposite sides of the table, avoiding each other's eyes.

|| || || At 7:00, I'm in the bathroom shaving before school. My face has broken out again. The electric razor whines as I twist it around zits.

Yellow pus oozes from one that's popped. I squeeze it until only watery blood remains and pat it with a piece of toilet paper.

"Move it, Miles," Mom calls.

I pull on my white jersey and look in the mirror. Zits on both cheeks. Who'd want to go out with me? I look like a clown.

"Mom, what's your favorite song in *Cats*?" Martha cuts her poached egg.

"'Memory.' What's yours?"

"'Jellicle Songs for Jellicle Cats.' I love that song. I think *Cats* is the best musical ever. Don't you, Miles?"

"Oh, definitely. I think it's the best musical in the entire musical history of musicals." I unwrap a breakfast bar.

"Miles, don't start the day with sarcasm." Mom's wearing her new blue suit. She must have a big meeting at the United Way.

Martha points at my jersey. "You look nice. Are you going to win tonight?"

"Yeah. Deer Rapids isn't any good."

"Don't be overconfident," Mom warns. "Your dad said to listen to your coaches."

I open the fridge for some orange juice. Dad's telling me what to do even when he's not here.

■■ ■■ ■■ At school, kids screw around in the hall before first period. Sam Hunter throws an empty water bottle, and a bunch of soccer players push to kick it.

"You might call it soccer, but most of the world calls it football," Sam says. "You guys are footballers."

Blue and white streamers decorate the lockers of varsity players. Each has a sign that's been painted by the cheerleaders. Mine says: HUNT THE BUCKS.

For home games, we wear our white jerseys to school, so it's easy to spot teammates. Brooksy walks down the hall with Megan Harkin. She's wearing his blue road jersey. She's tall, blond, and the best player on the tennis team. Brooksy is ripped. Together, they're a sharp-looking couple.

"Hey, Miles," she says.

"Hey, Megan." I grab my A.P. history book.

"Ready for Deer Rapids?" Brooksy asks.

"Yeah, we'll destroy 'em."

The buzzer sounds and we scatter.

▌▌ ▌▌ ▌▌ "I know there's a football game tonight and everybody is excited, but that's tonight. Right now we're going to study some history." Mr. Halloran stands at the podium and points to the board. "Let's explore immigration to America."

I look over at Megan. I'd love to go out with her. Someone hot. Someone wearing my jersey so everyone knows she's going with me. I can talk to girls okay, but I'm afraid to take the next step. I'd be crushed if I asked someone out and she said no. Who'd want to go out with me anyway?

"Why else did people come to America?" Halloran is looking at me. "Miles."

I say the first thing that pops into my mind. "Adventure."

Halloran writes it on the board underneath "economic opportunity" and "religious freedom."

"Some people came for adventure, but most people didn't leave their homes for that. Often, something forced them to go. What's another reason?"

Everybody looks around blankly. A new girl raises her

hand. She has dark curly hair and sits tall. "To avoid going to war," she says.

"Very good, Lucia." Halloran writes it down. "Many immigrants were escaping conscription into European armies. It's not something we talk about much, but America has a long tradition of providing a home for draft resisters."

I never heard that before. Is it true? I look over at Lucia. Silver bracelets jangle on her wrist as she writes in her notebook.

"For Wednesday," Halloran says, "talk with your parents about where your ancestors came from and why they came to America. Some of you may go back five or six generations. Some of you, it will be more recent. Talk with your mother and father and write down your answers."

Great. Homework. Homework that means talking with Dad about family.

Thanks a lot, Halloran.

chapter four

■ ■ ■ The lights are bright. The stadium's full. The pep band is playing "Come Together." A warm evening — perfect for football. Everybody's pumped to finally have a game. I stand next to Zach as Coach Sepolski finishes his pregame talk.

"You've seen the polls. You know we're ranked third in the state. Yes, we've got a chance to be a good football team. Yes, we've got a chance to go to State. But it's only a chance. If you want to make it a reality, you have to start here." Sepolski takes off his cap and wipes a towel across his bald head. "Play hard. Play smart. Let's have some fun."

"Fire up." Zach pounds my pads as we run onto the field. I jump over the white sideline for good luck. We both have eye black smeared under our eyes for the glare. I also like it because it makes me look tough.

"Corners and outside backers, over here," Sepolski calls. Brooksy, Krause, Zach, and I crowd close. "Remember, Deer Rapids likes to crackback on the quick pitch."

A crackback comes from the outside. If you don't see the block coming, it can destroy you as you turn.

Sepolski diagrams the block on his whiteboard. "Corners, shout out 'crackback.' Linebackers, you have two choices. One, turn away from it, take the hit in the back, and the ref will call a penalty. Two, avoid the block and fill outside. Zach and Miles, call it out."

We both nod.

Sepolski puts his fist out and we all put ours on top. "One, two, three," he says.

"Eagles," we yell together.

My stomach's flipping cartwheels as I scan the crowd. Mom, Dad, and Martha are sitting up by the press box. Mom and Martha wave and I lift my arm like I'm stretching. Dad tells them something. Probably to quit waving. He believes players should concentrate on the game.

"Manning, fly full speed, under control," Sepolski says. "You've got contain."

Contain's simple — run straight and don't get sucked in — but I'm still nervous. I tighten the Velcro on my gloves and take a deep breath.

The referee blows his whistle. Adams kicks off, and I run as hard as I can. Number 45 in red lowers his shoulder, but I fake inside and cut outside. The return man runs the other way and is tackled at the twenty-five.

The full moon rises above the concession stand, and the smell of hot dogs blends with cut grass. With the lights shining, I feel like I'm onstage. On the first play, the quarterback pitches to the tailback and the wideout cracks down.

"Crackback," I holler. Krause turns to avoid the blocker. I rush to hold the end as the pulling guard charges like a bull escaping the rodeo. I know the running back will cut in off the guard's block, so at the last moment I lunge left. My shoulder hits his knee and turns him over.

"Good hit, Man." Krause slaps my back.

"Way to call it out, Miles," Sepolski shouts.

Suddenly the crowd, the lights, the cartwheels in my stomach disappear. That first solid hit puts me in a different place. Time slows and I focus on what's in front of me.

The wideout lines up with his hands by his face like he's a boxer. As if this will make him faster. I want to knock him out already. He looks to the middle of the field twice. My gut says pass, and I doubt their quarterback has the balls to go long on the second play of the game. I slide up to take away the slant.

"Hut one, hut two." The quarterback drops.

"Pass," linebackers holler.

The ball comes right at me. I take a step, catch it, and run for the end zone. Wide-open green field. Nobody can touch me as I fly for the score. I hold the ball over my head and hand it to the ref.

The crowd goes crazy. "Interception return for a touchdown by Number 42, Miles Manning," crackles over the speakers. The band launches into "We Will Rock You." Perfect way to start the season.

Brooksy gives me a chest bump. "Way to go, Man."

Zach slaps me on the helmet. "You got one. I'll get one, too." He's all jacked up.

We sit on the bench, and I watch the cheerleaders shake their pom-poms. Kyra Richman sees me staring and waves. She looks good in her short skirt.

Everything clicks for us tonight. Our defense dominates. Stillwell chews up yards at fullback. Jonesy throws three touchdown passes. In the third quarter, Zach rips the ball away from the tight end for our second interception. By then the score is 35–3, and Coach Sepolski puts in the subs.

"Turner, Manning, over here," two boys behind the bench call. I wave, but Zach ignores them.

"Way to go, Miles," one of them says.

After the game, the locker room is loud. Jonesy shoots an old jock at me. I sneak up behind him and shove it in his face.

"That's so gay," he says.

"What do you have for paint?" Zach shows me the red on his helmet.

"I've got more than that." I show him two smears from a couple of helmet-to-helmet hits in the second quarter.

"Smart play on that interception, Miles." Coach Sepolski shakes my hand. "Great players make great plays at crucial times."

"Thanks, Coach." The adrenaline's rushing through my body. We *can* be really good this year.

Then Coach Stahl comes over. "Don't get too excited, men. We've still got work to do." He rubs his mustache. "Deer Rapids ran some traps to set up that field goal in the second quarter."

Is he serious? "Yeah, Coach. We'll try to play better next week."

Stahl turns and his mouth tightens. "I don't need any smart-ass comments, Manning. You've got plenty of room for improvement and so does this whole team. The minute you think you've got it all figured out, that's the minute you're in trouble."

We just won 45–3. I can't believe Stahl won't let us enjoy it.

"You shouldn't be satisfied unless you hold the

opponent to zero. If they score, you should be thinking about what you did wrong."

I look at the floor and hope he's finished.

"More concentration, Manning. Let's see if you can go out next week and hold Clifton scoreless."

"Okay, Coach." I pull off my pads.

Stahl swaggers into the coaches' room. What a jerk.

"Hurry up, Man," Zach says. "Party time."

chapter five

■■ ■■ ■■ Izzy's is packed by the time we get there. Every spot is taken, so we end up parking two blocks away in front of the beauty school.

"Confluence is number one," the driver of a Jeep shouts. Kids wave foam number one hands out the windows.

"Way to go, Eagles. Way to go," six senior girls sing as the driver hits her horn.

Zach orders two bacon cheeseburgers with fries. I get a fish sandwich, onion rings, and a strawberry malt. We sit outside to watch the show.

"You guys look ready for the play-offs," Strangler says. He's the starting center on the basketball team. "You both got interceptions. Manning got a touchdown, though, while Turner just fell down."

"Shove it, Strangler." Zach gives him a push.

Brooksy and Megan join us.

"Good game." Megan smiles at me.

"Thanks."

"What was Stahl talking about?" Brooksy unwraps a cheeseburger.

"How the defense shouldn't be satisfied if we give up points." I hold my thumb and finger to form zero.

"I thought we played great." Brooksy takes a big bite.

"Stahl's pissed we were celebrating, rather than concentrating on the three points we gave up." I dip an onion ring in Zach's ketchup. "Can you believe it?"

"He wants us to get better," Zach says. "Coaches always talk that way." Zach likes Stahl. He's taken weight training from him twice.

"Sepolski doesn't." I crumple my wrapper and throw it at the trash.

"Sepolski's different," Zach says. "Most coaches aren't like him."

"I know, but why's Stahl always on me?"

"You think too much," Zach says. "Stahl doesn't like that. He wants you to do it his way."

"What if there's a better way?" I hold a spoonful of malt upside down to see if it'll stay on.

"That's what he doesn't like, players thinking about a better way."

"Homecoming is in four weeks." Megan changes the subject. "Are you going to the dance, Zach?"

"Yup." He nods.

"With who?"

"You'll have to wait and see."

"How about you, Miles?" Megan turns her blue eyes to me. "Are you going?"

"I'm not sure." The malt slides off the spoon. I want to talk about something else.

"You should go," Megan says. "It'll be fun."

"Party at the Quarry." Zach checks his messages as we walk to the truck. "Two kegs. Sophomore girls. Let's go."

"Nah, I'm ready to go home." Kyra won't be there, and I don't feel like drinking.

"You sure?"

"Yeah." Zach and I signed the Conduct Code agreeing not to drink, smoke, or take drugs. Last year, we followed it together. This year's already different.

"Who're you asking to the dance?" I drum my fingers on the armrest on the ride home.

"Kate Meyer."

"Nice." Kate Meyer's a gorgeous sophomore who recently broke up with her senior boyfriend. She likes to party. She's probably at the Quarry now.

"Who're you going to ask?" Zach turns onto my street.

"I was thinking about Kyra Richman."

"She's hot. Not going out with anybody. She likes stars." Zach and I bump fists. "You played like a star tonight. That Blast helped jack you up."

"Yeah." I'd forgotten about the capsules. I'm not sure I want to start with that stuff. Besides, I played great.

What difference does it make if Zach thinks I took them when I didn't?

ll   ll   ll   Dad's watching ESPN Classic when I walk in, even though it's after midnight. I don't know how he does it. He gets up at 5:00, works all day, and stays up late. That doesn't seem human.

"Did you lock the door behind you?" he asks.

"Yeah."

"Are you sure?"

"Positive."

"Did you listen to your coaches?"

"Yeah."

"That Deer Rapids is one bad-looking team. Undersized, slow, totally predictable on offense. What a disorganized bunch." Sometimes Dad likes to talk football, and after a win I can listen. "That trap caused some problems, though. What those ends need to do is go low, submarine the blocker, and come right back up in front of the tailback. That'll shut it down."

"Yeah." Dad used to play defensive end. He's six foot five and weighed 260 pounds in high school. He was the star of his high school team and started in college until he broke his leg senior year. He knows his football.

"When the play goes the other way, make sure you

cover your area." Dad diagrams it with his hands. "You can move with the play, but be ready to get back on a reverse or a counter. There was a play in the third quarter when you got sucked over. If they'd swung it back, they'd have scored."

He sounds like Stahl. Why's he always have to focus on the negative? "How about my interception?"

"Yeah, you were in position, but that quarterback doesn't have much of an arm, does he?"

"No." I can tell this is about as much as I'm going to get. "Good night, Dad."

"Night." He turns up the volume.

Before falling asleep, I replay my interception. Stepping up. Grabbing the ball. Starting the year with a touchdown. Kyra saw that. Maybe she *will* say yes if I ask her. I'd love to kiss her. I wonder if I'd kiss okay.

For practice, I lean over and kiss my wrist, as if I were kissing Kyra's lips. I'd like to do more than kiss her. I picture that as I drift into the state between sleep and awake.

chapter six

▌▌ ▌▌ ▌▌ When I get up, Mom's typing on her laptop and Martha's watching Scooby-Doo. "That was a fun game last night," Mom says. "You played well."

"Thanks." I fill a bowl with Frosted Flakes and find the sports section. "Eagles Pick Off Bucks" is the headline. Underneath is a picture of my interception. "Eagles star Miles Manning intercepts a pass and returns it thirty-one yards for the opening touchdown."

Kyra will see that. Dad will, too.

"Manning's interception got us going," Coach Sepolski says in the article. "That was a good first game, our best in years. This team has the potential to be something special." I read the story three times to remember the good parts.

"Look, Mom." I show her the picture.

"How exciting," she says. "We'll send a copy to Grandma."

"What is it?" Martha hurries over. "Number 42. That's you, Miles. I'll call Grandma."

"Mom, can I ask you some homework questions?" I place my bowl and spoon in the dishwasher.

"Sure. Let me finish this first." Her fingers fly across the keyboard.

"What about me?" Martha says. "Don't you have questions for me?" Grandma must not have been home.

"Oh yeah, I've got a whole set." I pick up a blank piece of paper and study it.

Martha gets her Hello Kitty pad and pencil. "I'm ready."

"Number one, what's the best musical of all time?"

"That's easy. *Cats.*" Martha writes it down.

I stare at my paper. "Number two, what's the second-best musical of all time?"

"That's harder. I would say either *Beauty and the Beast* or *The Lion King.*"

"If you were held over hot, burning coals until you had to choose, which would it be?"

"What kind of hot, burning coals?"

"Lava. Molten lava, two thousand degrees."

"Celsius or Fahrenheit?" Martha asks.

"What difference does it make? Just answer the question."

"*The Lion King.*" She writes it down. "*Beauty and the Beast* would be third."

"Now, for the most important question. Who is the best brother in the world?"

Martha leans over to see. "That's not a real question."

"It's as real as any of them." I pull the paper away.

"The best brother in the world. Kurt." Martha writes it down.

"Who?"

"Kurt in *The Sound of Music*. He's nice to Marta and Gretl. He never makes up fake homework questions. Yup, Kurt is the best brother in the world."

"In that case, Smart Pants, your interview is over. The correct answer to the last question is Number 42, Miles Manning."

"No, it's not." Martha circles the answer on her paper. "It's Kurt."

▌▌ ▌▌ ▌▌ Mom's gone outside to pull weeds from her geranium pots.

"Ready for some questions?"

"Sure." She digs among the plants.

"Where did your ancestors come from and why did they come to America?"

"Well, my dad's family came from Poland and my mom's came from Germany."

I write this down. "Why did they come?"

"For opportunity, I guess. You should call Drew. He knows all that stuff." Mom's brother, Drew, is a librarian in Boston and lives with his partner, Stephen. "Drew's researched the family history," she says. "His number is in my address book on the desk."

"Can't you call him?" I pick at my thumbnail.

"It's your homework, Miles."

I haven't seen Drew or Stephen since Grandma's seventieth birthday, two years ago. Dad offered them fruit salad and made a big deal about the pansies in the window box. Nobody told him to stop and Stephen got angry. "I could send him an e-mail."

"Miles, go get Drew's number." Mom points with her trowel. "Call him."

I find the number and dial it. Maybe nobody will be home. "Hello, Drew?"

"This isn't Drew. It's Stephen. I'll get Drew."

That's bad. It's hard with two guys, but I should know my uncle's voice. Do Drew and Stephen think I thought Dad was funny at the party? I pace around the porch and bite my thumbnail.

"Hello?"

"Hello, Drew. It's Miles Manning."

"Hi, Miles. It's been a while. How are you doing?"

"Okay. Drew, I've got some homework. Mom said you could help." I open my notebook on the counter.

"What kind of homework?"

"Immigration. I need to know where my ancestors came from and why they came to America."

"Well, different branches of the family came for different reasons. Grandpa Zaleski and Grandma, who was a

Kaczmarek, came from southern Poland. Grandpa came because he had an older brother here. Grandma came to marry Grandpa."

I'm writing as fast as I can while Drew talks.

"On my mom's side, my grandma was Sofie Schmidt, who married Max Steinmitz. They'd grown up within twelve miles of each other in Germany but never met. Sofie came over with her older brother Joachim. He left Germany because he didn't want to be drafted. Your great-grandfather Max came to avoid conscription, too."

Just like Halloran said. I can't believe it. "Drew, how do you know all this stuff?"

"I've done some research and been over to Germany and Poland. It's important for me to know where we're from."

"Thanks, Drew." I look at my page full of notes.

"No problem, Miles. Say hi to everyone, and call again."

"Okay, I will."

That was easier than I thought. I can't imagine it will go that well with Dad.

chapter seven

▮▮ ▮▮ ▮▮ Dad picks basil in his garden Saturday evening. As big as he is, he moves easily among the plants. He's whistling "When Irish Eyes Are Smiling," so this is as good a time as any to ask my questions.

"How were things at the store today?"

"Lousy. Wal-Mart's killing us. People will drive all over creation to save fifty cents on a gallon of paint."

Mistake number one: Don't ask about work. "There's a picture of my interception in the paper. Coach says we have the potential to be something special."

"Don't be drooling over the paper. That game's over. You need to prepare for the next one." Dad puts the basil in a plastic bag. "Potential's just potential. Wait until the end of the season to see how special this team is."

Mistake number two: Don't fish for a compliment. I should know that by now. "How's the basil?"

"Pretty good. It likes this heat."

"Dad, I've got some homework questions. I already asked Mom, and she had me call Drew."

"Oh, Drew, the brilliant Drew. To hear your mother tell it, he's on the verge of being nominated for a Nobel Prize for being an all-around genius."

Mistake number three: Don't mention Drew.

"You better be careful talking to him. He might recruit you for the fruit team." Dad twists a tie on the bag.

"C'mon, Dad. Can we start with the questions?"

"What are they?" He picks an eggplant and sets it on the grass.

"Where did the people in your family come from and why did they come to America?"

"They were all Irish. My great-grandfather Manning came from county Wicklow." Dad stands up and points to an imaginary map of Ireland. "On my mother's side, they were famine Irish from county Cork. They came in the 1840s because they were starving. And don't let anyone tell you there wasn't food in Ireland." His voice gets louder. "There was food. The British took it and left the Irish to starve."

I'm writing quickly. He makes it sound like the famine happened yesterday.

"Those British ran every country they colonized the same way — for the benefit of Britain. The United States had the sense to get rid of them early. The places they stayed, like India and Ireland, went through hell before they kicked them out. They're still trying to get rid of them in Ireland."

"So what should I put for the reasons they came?" I flip to a new page in my notebook.

"Do you have wax in your ears?" he shouts. "They were starving. They didn't have enough to eat."

■■ ■■ ■■ On Sunday, I check the computer at Easy Rest Mattress to see what Zach sold yesterday. Three queen sets, a king, and two twins. I'd better sell some stuff to keep up with him.

Sunday mornings are slow, so the manager has me open the store by myself. The bell rings and I glance up. A woman with red-spiked hair takes off her sunglasses. She's wearing a tank top and a tiny skirt.

"Hi. Can I help you?" My voice comes out shaky.

"I need a new queen-size mattress. My old one's shot." She clips her glasses to her tank top and I peek at them. It's easy to imagine her wearing out a mattress.

"What's the box spring like?" I ask.

"What?" She's in her twenties. That's not too old.

"The box spring. Underneath the mattress. How's your box spring?"

"I don't know." She raises her eyebrows like I'm asking her something personal.

"If you put a new mattress on an old box spring, the mattress will wear out faster. You're better off getting a new set."

"You sure know a lot about beds. You must have a lot of experience." She winks.

What should I do? Ask her name? Get her phone number? Instead, I explain coil counts and what's inside the box spring.

She runs her hand over a mattress in the corner. "I like this one. The pink flowers are pretty."

I don't tell her that once the sheets are on, nobody'll see the pattern. I'm excited to have this woman stand close while I punch in the order. I breathe in her sexy perfume. I wish I was more like Zach. He'd know what to say.

As the woman drives away in her Miata, I imagine going out with her. She's probably got her own place. She's got her fun car and a new bed. I need to quit dreaming. I need to find the guts to ask Kyra out. I read someplace that the average sixteen-year-old guy thinks about sex once every seven seconds. I've been thinking about it more.

Since there are no other customers, I go back to the factory part of the store where we make mattresses to order. I think about the woman winking as I lift a six-sixty-coil innerspring onto the table. I pull a piece of Typar, the gray mesh fabric, from the roll. I tuck it under the corners and pick up the hog ringer. *Chunnc*, the power gun makes a solid sound as it drives a ring around the coil to hold the Typar. I put a foam topper over that and tuck it into the corners.

On the wall, beneath the clock, is a calendar from Leggett & Platt, the innerspring supplier, with a picture of a father and son in a canoe. Dad and I used to do stuff like that. I remember our first trip on the Bow River when I was seven. We went with Sully, who works for Dad, and his son Jeremy. I'd never been in a canoe before, and I loved sitting in the middle as we floated on the water.

For lunch, we stopped at a sandbar in the middle of the river. We sat on a log and ate peanut butter sandwiches, Sun Chips, and Fruit Roll-Ups. Jeremy and I drank Kool-Aid and the men drank beer. Afterward, I waded in a shallow pool and tried to catch tiny fish as they darted between my legs.

In the late afternoon, as we sang paddling songs, the current got stronger. The sun dipped behind a hill, and it cooled down. We came around a bend. A tree had fallen all the way across the river. We were headed straight for it.

"Steer to the right." Dad paddled hard. "There's a gap."

"Jeremy, Miles, bend down," Sully yelled.

I ducked to avoid leaves and branches. The canoe smashed something solid.

"A rock," Dad shouted. The canoe spun sideways, wobbled a few seconds, then tipped over.

Suddenly I was beneath the surface. I opened my eyes but couldn't see. I didn't know where anybody was. Cold water surrounded me. I kicked and swam wildly. Then I felt a strong hand grab me and pull me to the surface. I came up under the canoe.

"Hang on to this bar," Dad said.

Moments later, he came back up with Jeremy. He saved both of us. Afterward, he told me not to say anything to Mom because she'd worry. We never talked about it again.

The phone rings. "Easy Rest Mattress — remember the name; the rest is easy."

"Depends who you're resting with," Zach says. "I talked to Kate. She said yes. Then she sent me a picture message of herself in her new bikini."

"Wow."

"Have you asked Kyra yet?"

"I'm working on it." I walk over to the empty table and sit down.

"Well, quit working on it and do it."

"Yeah, I will. A woman who looked like a model was in here flirting with me."

"Did you ask her to the dance?"

"No, she's not in high school."

"You've always got an excuse," Zach says. "Talk to Kyra."

"Don't worry. I will. Bye."

I go back to the mattress and pull the cover over the foam. It's easy for Zach to ask Kate. He's good-looking. He drives a new truck. He's got lots of girls who want to go out with him. I've got a fresh zit on my chin. I'd have to ask Mom to borrow her old Civic. And I don't know if Kyra would say yes.

II II II We watch game tapes Sunday night in the small gym at school. Zach and I grab folding chairs from the cart and set them next to each other. Everybody's in a good mood after the win.

Sepolski pauses the tape on my interception. "You D-backs, watch how Manning takes away the slant and jumps the ball. That's smart football."

Getting a compliment from Coach in front of the team always feels good.

Someone farts loudly in back.

"Is that you, Jonesy?" Sepolski asks.

"Yes, Coach. I'm having digestive problems."

"You're the Superstar." Laughter echoes in the room.

Then Stahl takes over and focuses on the trap. He runs it over and over telling us how to recognize it, defend it, and stop it. "What do we want to hold our opponents to?"

"Zero," we say.

"What?"

"ZERO."

"That's better."

■■ ■■ ■■ At practice Tuesday, second offense is going against first defense. Fox, the backup quarterback, dings his finger on a helmet and goes to the trainer. Jonesy, the starter, comes in to replace him.

"Down, set, hit." Someone jumps offside.

"Pay attention," Sepolski snaps. "Run one play right, and we're out of here."

"Down, set, hit." Jonesy drops back to pass, and I cover Stillwell in the flat. Tyson Ruden, the tackle, breaks free.

"Go get him, big fella," Sepolski hollers.

Tyson grabs Jonesy, spins him like a doll, and flings him to the ground.

"You okay, Fox?" Coach calls. Jonesy is crumpled up holding his right shoulder. "Fox, are you hurt?"

37

"It's not Fox," I say. "It's Jonesy."

"No, no!" Sepolski runs over. "Jonesy, are you okay?"

Jonesy grimaces and shakes his head. Coach Stahl runs in and blows the whistle. "Break it up, men. Hit the weights."

I walk in with Zach. "I can't believe Coach sent Tyson after Jonesy."

"Let's hope it's not bad," Zach says.

chapter eight

■■ ■■ ■■ It's bad. Jonesy has a separated shoulder. So bad, he's out for the season.

"Jonesy didn't come to school today," Zach says.

"Can you blame him? Would you after your season's been destroyed because Coach sent Tyson after you?"

"Coach didn't know it was Jonesy."

"I know." I slam my locker. "But that doesn't help him. That doesn't help us."

The buzzer sounds and I hurry to history.

"Take out your homework," Halloran says. I arrange my notes on my desk. I can't imagine Jonesy being out. Since middle school, he's been the leader. I feel a surge of fear. Who's our leader now?

"Okay," Halloran says. "Give me some reasons your ancestors came to America."

"To have their own land."

"To give their kids a better life."

"To join other family members."

Kids are shouting out answers and Halloran's writing them on the board.

"To escape religious persecution."

"To dodge the draft," Strangler says. Everybody laughs

because Strangler's a skinny guy who wouldn't be much good in a fight.

"Let's see some hands," Halloran says. "How many of you had at least one ancestor come to this country to avoid fighting in a war?"

I raise my hand along with a few other kids.

"How many of your parents said they didn't know why their ancestors came to this country?"

Lots of kids raise their hands. Thanks to Drew, I don't have to.

Halloran leans on his podium. "Sometimes the reasons people came to America were not the most noble: to escape debts, to avoid prosecution, to skip responsibility after getting someone pregnant. There can be all kinds of reasons. Some of you might want to investigate further. Why your ancestors came to this country is important. It helps connect you with who you are." Halloran turns back to the board. "Okay, what's another reason people came to America?"

The new girl raises her hand. "Love," she says.

Halloran writes "love" on the board. "Can you give us an example, Lucia?"

"My grandfather was an American soldier in Germany. He went to Italy to see frescoes in Ravenna and met my grandmother. They fell in love, got married, and she moved to America with him."

"Yes, people do all kinds of things for love," Halloran says. Some of the girls smile. "What's another reason?"

"Because they were starving," I blurt out.

Halloran writes "starvation" on the board. "Where was it, Miles?"

"Ireland, during the famine. My dad says there was food, but the British took it."

"He's right. The famine was caused by more than the potato blight. Millions of Americans, including me, are descendants of Irish who came to this country so they'd have enough to eat."

The room is quiet as we listen to Halloran. He's the only teacher I have who links the past with the present. Right now, desperate people in Ireland, lovers in Italy, and draft dodgers in Germany feel like they're here with us.

"Remember this, the next time somebody complains about immigrants from Mexico, Africa, or Asia," Halloran says. "Remember, the reasons these immigrants are coming are the same ones your ancestors had."

Halloran turns and points to the board. "There's one group who didn't come to America for any of these reasons. For Friday, write down who that was and why none of these reasons apply."

■ ■ ■ At practice, Coach Sepolski follows the usual routine, but everybody's thinking about Jonesy. Fox struggles to run first offense. He fumbles snaps. He misreads keys. He misses wide-open receivers. But worst of all, he's got no zip on his passes. The ball floats like a dead duck.

When we split up by position, Coach Stahl pulls a few guys, including Zach, to try out for quarterback. He doesn't ask me, even though I've got a decent arm. I'd like to be asked, but I wouldn't want to switch. I love defense. I love being the hitter, rather than the hittee.

Afterward, I ask Zach about the tryout. "How'd it go?"

"Not great," he says. "Stillwell looked good, though."

Stillwell's the starting fullback. He's got a strong arm. There's no way he's Jonesy, and we'd need a new fullback, but that might work.

"Besides," Zach says, "I told Coach I need to stay on defense to look after you."

■ ■ ■ Zach and I swing by Jonesy's on the way home. Jonesy's got his arm in a sling and is watching beach volleyball on TV. Football magazines cover the floor.

"We brought you something, Star." I pull out a box of Twinkies.

"Thanks." Jonesy keeps his eyes on the screen. Normally, he loves junk food.

"I'd like to play with her." Zach points to a blonde spiking the ball.

"Dream on," Jonesy says.

"We miss you bad, Star," I say. "Fox was terrible." I don't know if this helps, but Jonesy's paying attention now.

"They should try Stillwell," Jonesy says.

I look over at Zach, who nods.

Jonesy clicks off the TV. "The defense has to dominate. You've got to be monsters. The offense will be okay, but the defense can win games." He's still thinking about the team. It's part of what makes him such a good quarterback.

"Tyson feels bad," Zach says.

"He should have eased up." I open a Twinkie and hand it to Jonesy.

"That's Tyson," Jonesy says. "He was rushing. Coach was yelling. Maybe he didn't know it was me." He takes a bite of the Twinkie.

"He's played with you for two years," I say. "He should know."

"Don't blame Tyson," Zach says. "We've got to stick together."

Sometimes I wish Zach didn't sound so much like a

coach. I wish he'd think for himself more. I hand Jonesy another Twinkie. "You've still got senior year. You're still the Superstar."

"That's right. It's not like I'm dead." Jonesy shoves the Twinkie into his mouth.

■■ ■■ ■■ At home, I stare out my bedroom window. I don't like seeing Jonesy in that sling.

"Miles." Mom knocks.

"Yeah."

She hurries in and shuts the door. "I found these in your pocket when I was doing laundry." She holds the gold capsules. "What are they?"

"Nothing." I cross my arms.

"What?" She looks worried.

"Something one of the guys gave me. It's nothing." How stupid to leave them in my pocket.

"What are they?" She shuts off my CD player.

"I didn't take them."

"Why are they here?" Mom paces back and forth.

"Because I didn't take them. That's why they're in my pocket."

Mom's eyes narrow with the look she gets when she's angry. "I'm asking you once more what these are," she says. "If you don't tell me, I'll call your father."

That's one thing I don't need. "They're called Rip Blast."

"What's that?"

"Just caffeine. Something guys take to get psyched up."

"Who gave them to you?"

"Zach."

"Is he taking them?" She looks closely at the pills, as if she's expecting them to talk.

"Yeah. It's nothing."

"Don't mess with these, Miles." She runs her hand through her hair. "I read an article in *People* about a high school football player who committed suicide after taking steroids. It devastated his family."

"These aren't steroids, Mom." Sometimes she's so extreme.

"I don't want you taking anything. Don't risk your future for a football game."

"Okay, Mom."

"Stay away from them. Do you understand?"

"Yes, Mom."

"Do you promise?"

"*Yes*, Mom."

She stands at the door as if she wants to say more.

"You're not telling Dad, are you?"

"I don't know. Do you think I need to?" She rubs her lower lip.

"No."

"I'll see." Mom closes the door.

I hear the toilet flush and imagine the capsules swirling down.

I'm not sure how Dad would react. He wants me to be a better football player, but he doesn't like drugs. This isn't really a drug, though. It's a stimulant, a performance enhancer. But Dad doesn't like shortcuts either.

chapter nine

▌▌ ▌▌ ▌▌ "Jonesy has a separated shoulder and is out for the season." I get right to the news at dinner.

"What?" Dad asks. "How'd Sepolski get his quarterback hurt in practice?"

"He didn't know it was Jonesy."

"How could he not know?"

"He thought it was Fox."

"He can't keep his quarterbacks straight. Maybe he's losing it."

I take some salad and pass it to Martha.

"Perhaps it was an accident," Mom says.

"Accident!" Dad snorts. "An accident is something you can't control. A coach is supposed to be in control. Sepolski should know who's quarterback."

How come Dad tells me to respect my coaches, but he gets to say what he wants about them? How come I don't get that freedom?

"The lasagna's delicious," Martha says.

"Yeah, Mom, it's good." I don't think she told Dad about the capsules.

"Kelsey said her sister is going to the homecoming dance." Martha looks at me. "Are you going, Miles?"

"I don't know. I'm thinking about it."

"You don't need that crap," Dad says. "You've got football, school, your job. That's plenty. I've seen too many guys get so wrapped up in girls that they let football and homework go to hell. You'll have plenty of time for that later."

What does he know? Why can't he lighten up?

"I'm sure there are nice girls who haven't been asked who would love to go." Mom's concept of dating has no connection to the real world. "What about that Ritter girl?" Stephanie Ritter is on the chess team and hardly talks. "I'm sure no one has asked her."

"I'm sure no one has either."

"What do you mean?" Mom asks. "She's nice."

"Let's drop this whole damn subject." Dad raises his voice. "I already said Miles has plenty going on. He can wait."

I push bits of noodle around my plate. Dad's not in charge of my life. It's not his decision. Why can't he just shut up?

∎ ∎ ∎ Coach Sepolski gathers the defensive starters. "As you know, Jonesy's out for the season. Josh Stillwell's our new quarterback. It will take a while for him to adjust to the position. In the meantime, the defense has to step up."

I scrape dirt off my cleats with a stick and try not to think about Jonesy.

"We're at Clifton tomorrow," Sepolski says. "Let's have a strong practice to get ready."

We jog down to the goalpost to work on blitzes. Fox is running second offense, and I feel sorry for him. First Sepolski thought he was sending Tyson after him; then he gets yanked as a starter after one day.

Sepolski comes into our huddle. "Manning, run the corner blitz. Don't show it early. Wait for the right moment, then explode."

I creep up to the line, then back off a step when Fox looks over. "Down, set, hit." As soon as I see movement, I burst forward. Nobody picks me up and I've got a free shot at Fox.

Sepolski blows his whistle. "We don't need anybody else hurt. Hossick, where the hell are you? You've got to pick up the blitz. What are you doing, dreaming about your girlfriend?"

Sepolski slaps me on the shoulder. "Good work, Manning. Way to time it."

II II II During water break by the shed, I watch the offense. "Down, set, hit." Stillwell spins on a fake, then throws a tight pass to Brooksy in the flat. We're going to be okay.

Sepolski claps his hands. "Let's end with ten sprints.

Line up by position." I line up with the receivers and the defensive backs at the forty-yard line. Coach blows the whistle and we run hard. As usual, Zach finishes first and I'm in the middle. On the final sprint, Coach Stahl is barking, "Don't give up, men. Don't give up."

I push across the line and quietly say, "Oh, I give up."

"That's the problem with you, Manning." Stahl points. "You always give up. You look for the easy way out. You're too smart for your own good."

He turns to the linebackers. "Don't give up, men. Don't give up."

I have no idea why I said that. Maybe because the idea of sprinting four hundred yards and giving up on the final five seemed so idiotic. Who'd give up then? But why would I say it? Maybe I *am* too smart for my own good.

In the locker room, Zach shakes his head. "Why'd you do that?"

"I don't know. What Stahl said seemed so stupid. It just came out."

"Well, what you did was stupid."

I throw my helmet in my locker. I've got an empty feeling in my stomach, like everything's been sucked out. I sit on the bench with my head in my hands.

chapter ten

▌▌ ▌▌ ▌▌ On game day, my locker is decorated with a blue and white sign that says: JAIL THE PIRATES. Clifton is the Pirates, which makes no sense because they're nowhere near an ocean. They don't even have a lake. I like it when team names have something to do with the town. Deer Rapids, for example, being the Bucks shows they're trying. Pirates for Clifton is lame.

As I walk to Halloran's class, Kyra Richman laughs with her friends. Why do they always travel in a group? If she weren't surrounded all the time, I could talk to her.

In history, Halloran tells us to take out our homework. I forgot to do it. I rip out a piece of paper, write my name, and ask Strangler for the answer.

"Indians," he says. "Already here."

Halloran circles the room collecting papers. He looks at my blue jersey. "Big game tonight," he says. "Who are we playing, Miles?"

"Clifton."

Halloran pretends he's not into sports, but I know he and Coach Sepolski are friends. "We talked about reasons immigrants came to America." Halloran stands at the board. "What is the one group for whom none of these apply?"

Strangler raises his hand. "Indians."

"Let's explore this." That's one of Halloran's favorite expressions. "How many people wrote down 'Indians'?"

I raise my hand, along with most of the class.

"Why Indians, Miles?"

"Because they were already here."

"Yes," Halloran says. "Indians or Native Americans were here when Europeans arrived, and they'd been here for thousands of years. But had they always been here?"

Lisa Williams waves her hand wildly. "They came across the Bering Strait land bridge. I saw a show about it on the *National Geographic* Channel."

"That's one theory," Halloran says. "Many Indians don't agree, but most archaeologists believe that ancestors of Indians came here thousands of years ago. Why would they have come?"

"For food."

"For better hunting."

"For more land."

"Surprisingly, some of the same reasons that we listed on the board. There is one group, however, for whom *none* of these reasons apply."

Lucia raises her hand. "Slaves," she says softly, but we all hear.

"Yes," says Halloran. He pauses. In the silence it sinks in how obvious this is and how I missed it.

"Africans," Halloran says, "came to this country in chains and were sold as slaves. This is fundamentally different from any other group. They were forced to come here. They didn't choose to." While Halloran talks, I look around the room at the white faces.

"The trip to the Americas was called the Middle Passage," he says. "Research this and write a five-page paper for next Thursday."

■■   ■■   ■■   After lunch, Kyra dials her combination, and for once, she's alone.

"Hi, Kyra."

"Oh, hey, Miles."

"Bad news about Jonesy, isn't it?" I shift my books from one arm to the other and try to relax.

"Yeah, like it's bad, but I think we'll still be good." She doesn't seem too concerned. You'd think as a cheerleader she'd show more sympathy.

"Kyra."

"Yeah." She takes her books from her locker.

"Well, homecoming is coming home. I mean coming up. Homecoming is coming up in three weeks. Homecoming."

"Yes, Miles."

"I . . . was . . . wondering," I start out slow and then go fast, "if you'd go with me."

Kyra smiles her perfect orthodontist's daughter smile. "That's like sweet of you, Miles, but I'm already going with someone."

"Oh. Oh." I want to disappear. "Who? Who?" I sound like a lost owl.

"I'm going with Josh Stillwell." She tosses her hair back as she closes her locker. "He's the new quarterback, you know."

As if I didn't know who the quarterback was. As I walk away, five of Kyra's friends giggle by the drinking fountain.

chapter eleven

■■ ■■ ■■ The best thing about football is smashing into guys. After my total humiliation with Kyra, I can't wait to unload on a Pirate. On the bus, I sit next to Zach. He's already heard about Kyra shooting me down. Her friends wasted no time in spreading the news.

"That's why I waited," I say. "To pick the perfect time to be turned down."

"You can't find out if you don't ask."

"Yeah, right."

Zach reaches into his shirt pocket and takes out four capsules. He drops two onto my palm. "A little Blast. It'll help you play great again."

I remember my promise to Mom.

"Nothing to worry about." Zach slaps my thigh. "Gives you that aggressive edge. That's what wins games."

Zach's right. Football is about being aggressive, but I've never needed help with that. Zach puts the capsules in his mouth, takes a swig of water, and passes the bottle to me. I roll mine in my palm. Just caffeine, like drinking Red Bull. I pop them in my mouth, gulp some water, and swallow.

I look out the window at green fields of corn and wait

to feel different. Everything's the same. Mom doesn't need to know about it. She doesn't need to know everything I do.

Coach Sepolski gathers us in the locker room. "Clifton's a good football team and they're always tough at home. Fellas, this is your time. Set the tone of the game. Play hard. Play smart. Have fun." Coach's hand chops the air. "Dedicate this game to Jonesy. Go out and win it for him."

"Yeahhhhhh." The yell rips through the room. I'm ready to hit a Pirate so hard he'll have to hunt for his teeth. I want to push their tailback out of bounds and drive him into the metal fence that surrounds the field.

Coach shakes hands with each guy as we leave the locker room. We line up behind Jonesy, who leads us onto the field through a tunnel of screaming cheerleaders. Kyra Richman keeps her eyes on Josh Stillwell. I spit at her feet.

I grab Jonesy on the sideline. "I'll get you a Pirate." Is that the Blast or am I just psyched?

A roar rises from the crowd when we kick off. I sprint straight for a Pirate blocker and hit him as hard as I can. He crashes over backward.

"Reverse." The play's coming back my way. I've kept my contain lane, so the runner cuts in. I grab his white jersey and spin him around. The pursuit races in and we gang-tackle him at the twenty-one.

"Way to contain, Manning," Sepolski hollers.

On second and nine, Coach signals a blitz. I go up to the line, like I'm playing bump and run. When the quarterback looks over, I back off a couple of steps. He checks the other way. "Hut one."

I race in free. The quarterback's following a receiver on Zach's side. No one picks me up. I lower my shoulder and hammer him before his arm moves forward.

"Fumble." Tyson jumps on the ball.

Zach pounds me on the shoulder. "Way to lay a lick, Man."

Clifton coaches and trainers rush to check the quarterback.

"One Pirate for you, Superstar." I point to Jonesy as I bounce off the field.

"Awesome blitz, Man. I watched you all the way. That's one screwed-up Pirate." He pushes me with his good arm.

Our ball at the Clifton twelve. Nice way for Stillwell to start. Two running plays gain six. On third and four, Coach calls a pass to Brooksy in the flat.

"Down, set, hit." Stillwell spins and Brooksy is wide open. Stillwell tosses a strike. Touchdown.

"Yeahhh." We're rollin'. We're going to be okay.

Clifton brings in a new quarterback. I want Coach to call the blitz so I can knock him out, but we play it straight. Three downs and the Pirates punt.

We keep giving the offense good field position, and Stillwell looks sharp. At halftime we're up 21–0, and we roar into the locker room. "Let's hold them to zero," I shout. Coach Stahl nods.

Jonesy uses his left hand to diagram pass patterns for Stillwell. It must be hard for him not to be playing.

When we go up 28–0, Coach pulls first defense and puts in the second string. He stays with first offense, though. I'm sure he wants Stillwell to get more work with them.

"Watch the hook and go," Zach calls to Bachman, his backup.

"Tell them to sharpen their cutlasses," I yell. I'm still buzzing from the Blast.

Bachman looks confused and Zach waves him off. "Hook and go," he says.

Jonesy and I are pretending to swordfight when Coach Stahl notices. "Don't celebrate early," he says. We haven't given up any points, but he has to warn us about something. I'm glad to see Jonesy laughing.

On the first play of the fourth quarter, Stillwell drops

back on a center screen. It's a timing play, and he waits an extra second for Monson to get open. Stillwell plants to throw, and the Clifton end slams into his leg. Everyone on our bench stares in silence. Stillwell squirms in pain as coaches and trainers push to get to him.

Instantly the energy of the game changes. On their sideline, Pirate players exchange high fives. Celebrating someone getting hurt is wrong. Then I remember. That's exactly what I was doing with Jonesy in the first quarter.

Across the field, Dad stands along the fence. He hadn't told me he was driving all the way over here. He's shaking his head as Stillwell is wheeled to the ambulance. People in the stands clap politely. What are they clapping for? Relief their son isn't hurt?

Coach Stahl walks over. "That's why we don't celebrate early. Anything can happen in a football game."

Our celebrating had nothing to do with Stillwell getting hurt, but I don't respond. I look over at Jonesy, who's rubbing his eyes with his head down. Who's our quarterback now?

"Fox," Sepolski hollers. "Get in there."

chapter twelve

■ ■ ■   Zach leans over on the bus. "We gotta turn it up on D."

"Yeah." Maybe Stillwell's injury won't be serious, but from the way he was wheeled off, it looks bad. Two quarterbacks down. Going to State is going to be a lot harder. I bite my nails as we drive through the dark.

Zach and I swing by Izzy's. The usual crowd is there yelling and celebrating.

"Confluence rules," a girl in a blue Bug yells.

So many people don't know anything about football. They see 28–7 and think it's great. They have no idea that Stillwell getting hurt is worse than losing the game.

Strangler's saved us the booth in back. "How's Stillwell?"

"He's at the hospital in Clifton for X-rays." I don't feel hungry.

Jonesy comes over with a large Mountain Dew. "Bad news. Stillwell's leg is broken in two places."

"How'd you find out?" I slide over to make room.

"We called his house and his brother told us. He has to have a screw put in." Jonesy can't get the paper off his straw, so I rip it.

"Who'll be the new quarterback?" I look to Zach.

"I think it's Fox. Nobody else was any good in tryouts."

"What do you think, Jonesy?"

"If it's Fox, we're screwed."

"There's a party at Tyson's tonight," Zach says. "Let's check it out."

I remember Tyson shoving us around as freshmen. Maybe Zach's forgotten. "Who's going to be there?"

"Guys from the team. Sophomore girls."

"Let's go." Jonesy throws his cup at the trash with his left hand. "Depressing sitting here."

▌▌ ▌▌ ▌▌ Tyson greets us at the door holding a beer in one hand and a cigar in the other. "Grab a Bud, boys."

The living room is full of senior linemen eating Doritos and drinking beer. I knew Tyson partied after games, but I didn't know this many guys did.

"Hey, guys." Seniors greet us. We're the only juniors here.

Zach hands me a beer. "Drink up."

I twist off the cap.

"To Eagle football." Zach raises his Bud.

"To Eagle football." We clink bottles, and I take a swig of beer. I don't even like the taste.

At the dining room table, guys try to bounce quarters

into a glass of beer. Tyson's lands in the foam and he points to Jonesy.

"Chugalug, chugalug," they chant. Jonesy downs the beer.

Everybody seems to have forgotten about Stillwell. Maybe they haven't. Maybe they're scared about Fox being the quarterback. Maybe they're drowning their fear.

It's getting hot, so I pull off my sweatshirt. Zach grabs me around the shoulder and pulls me to the bathroom. "I've got something for you." He reaches into his pocket and pulls out a packet of pink pills.

"What's this?" I catch our reflection in the mirror. Zach looks confident. I look worried.

"D-Bol." He shakes one out for me.

"What?"

"Dianabol." He takes one for himself. "You'll put on five pounds in a week."

"I don't know." I look at the pill. How does something this tiny make you big?

"It works. You'll add muscle fast."

I need to be bigger. Five more pounds would help. Zach swallows his pill. "C'mon, Man."

I put mine in my mouth and wash it down with beer.

"Take three a day. Doctor's orders." Zach hands me the packet. "I'm getting another Bud. Want one?"

"Nah, I'm good."

In the living room, the DVD of *Gladiator* is playing. Each time a gladiator is injured, everyone drinks.

Strangler comes over. "No girls. Just football players drinking. I'm heading out."

"I'll go with you." I grab my sweatshirt. I wave to Zach as we leave. He gives me a thumbs-up while he, Jonesy, and Tyson drink to *Gladiator.*

■ ■ ■ When Strangler drops me off, I let myself in. Dad's snoring in the TV room. The volume's loud, but I don't dare turn it off. Instead, I tiptoe upstairs.

In bed, my mind bounces like a pinball. I close my eyes and see pink pills. I remember signing the Conduct Code with Dad before summer practice. Dad said, "You've given your word. Keep it." I broke it tonight. But so did a lot of guys. If that party got busted, we wouldn't have much of a team.

"Doctor's orders." Does Zach know what he's doing? Can I trust him on this? I turn on my light and go to the dresser. In the back of my underwear drawer is the packet. I examine the tiny pentagons. They look like little pink houses. Is it cheating to use them if other guys are?

I can't fall asleep. My body's exhausted, but my mind's wired. I see Stillwell plant his foot and the Clifton guy slam into his leg. That's how fast your season can end. Not just your season. That's how fast football can end.

I see myself smashing into the Pirate quarterback on my blitz. I still get a rush from hitting him that hard and causing the fumble. I wonder how he's doing?

One other scene: I'm at Kyra's locker asking her to the dance. Did that happen today? I see a dark drain and watch myself swirl down. Why did I think she'd go with me? "I'm going with Josh Stillwell," she says. "He's the new quarterback, you know."

Not anymore, Kyra. You're going to the dance with a guy on crutches.

■■   ■■   ■■ Mom and Martha are shooting hoops in the driveway Saturday morning. Mom shows Martha how to aim for the square on the backboard. Mom makes five in a row. She played in high school and still has a good shot. She's tall and thin. I'm built more like her than Dad.

I eat my cereal and look at the sports section. Underneath the headline "Eagles Lose Another QB" is a picture of Stillwell on the ground. Coach Sepolski says, "We have to dig down deep to see what we're made of." I don't know about digging deep. What we need is a healthy quarterback.

I go outside and call for the ball. Martha tosses it, and I launch a three pointer. Nothing but net.

"Nice shot," she says.

"Hold your left hand still." I demonstrate. "Your left hand just holds the ball. Push with your right hand. Hit the corner like Mom showed you, and it'll go in every time." I bank it in off the board.

Martha makes two in a row and jumps up and down. "That helps, Miles."

Mom turns to me. "Your dad wasn't happy after the game."

"Yeah, we lost another quarterback." My mind races. Is there anything else?

"Your dad forgot some printer software. He's coming by to pick it up." Sounds like a warning. She didn't tell him about the Blast, did she? Or did he find out about the party?

Martha rebounds for me and I make three jumpers in a row. I wipe my face with my T-shirt. It's already hot out.

Dad pulls in the driveway, and it takes one second to realize he's angry. He comes straight at me and seems bigger than his three hundred pounds. "That was a piss-poor performance last night."

"I know. Stillwell broke his leg in two places."

Mom and Martha pick up the ball and leave.

"I'm not talking about Stillwell. I'm talking about you. You make one play and spend the rest of the game screwing around. What were you doing dancing on the sideline with Jones?" He's pointing his finger in front of my face.

"I was trying to cheer him up."

"That's not your job. You looked like a couple of morons. Do you have any idea who was sitting behind me watching that crap?"

"No."

"Two college recruiters, the guys who give scholarships. They liked that first play of yours, but after that you didn't do a damn thing. Just pranced around the sideline. They noticed that, too."

I'm sure those scouts were watching Tyson, not me, but it's better to stay quiet.

"A college scholarship is worth a lot of money. I suppose you haven't thought about how to pay for college."

Dad's right. I haven't thought about it.

"When I played football, if we weren't serious, we got our butts kicked. If I pulled a stunt like that, my dad would have whipped me good."

I never knew my grandpa. It's hard for me to picture anyone whipping Dad.

"And why did Sepolski have Stillwell in there in the fourth quarter?"

"I don't know."

"Why the hell's he calling that center screen?"

"I don't know. He didn't ask me."

"That's the dumbest call he's made yet. Up by twenty-eight and running a center screen. Getting your quarterback hurt."

I nod my head and avoid eye contact.

"Don't let me catch you doing that crap on the sideline again. Next time, I'll come out of the stands and haul your ass out of there."

"Okay." I look at the laces of my shoes. Please let this end.

"Don't forget." Dad storms into the house.

chapter thirteen

■■ ■■ ■■ I don't want to be around when Dad's like this, so I walk downtown. He's always exploding. He takes something small and makes it huge. Why do I just stand there and take it? I cross over to Crescent to avoid going by the paint store. I don't want to see it.

Not much is happening downtown. Not much ever does. A woman in a flowery hat looks at romance novels outside the used bookstore. Drivers of matching PT Cruisers honk at the bank drive-through. Who'd drive a PT Cruiser? They look stupid.

The library overlooks the spot where the rivers come together. The AC will feel good, and I've got something to look up.

At the computer, I type my library card number and Google "Dianaball." Sounds like a girl's name.

It is. Diana Ball's a wrestler from Finland who's into weight lifting. That's not what I want.

I scroll down and click on Dianabol, the steroid. Up pops a picture of the pink pills. "Dianabol is an anabolic steroid used to produce rapid weight gain."

"GET HUGE AND SHREDDED IN NO TIME" flashes the banner. "Guaranteed to add fifteen pounds of pure muscle in three weeks." What football player wouldn't want that? It takes months of weight lifting to gain muscle. I'd love to speed it up. I'd look better for girls, too.

A box pops up for a free issue of the magazine *Testosterone Extra*. I type in my name and address and click the send button.

Another site describes "stacking," using multiple steroids for maximum growth. Charts show recommended dosages and schedules. "CLICK HERE FOR HOME DELIVERY." It's that easy?

When I go to sites that are not selling steroids, though, the information is different. "Steroids, which are artificial means to increase testosterone, may cause health problems. These include liver damage, cancer, shrinking testicles, reduced sperm count, severe acne, and impotence."

Zach didn't mention any of this. With that list of side effects, it's odd that the one I focus on is severe acne. Maybe because I've got bad skin. Impotence sounds bad, too. I don't want that.

When my computer time's up, I log off. Then I remember my homework for Halloran's class. The librarian at the reference desk looks helpful. "Do you have information on the Middle Passage?"

"That's not a request we get often." She glances up from her screen. "You're the second person to ask today."

Silver flashes in her mouth as she talks. She's got a tongue stud. "Is this for a class?"

"Yes. Who else asked?"

"A tall girl with dark curly hair, green eyes."

Sounds like Lucia.

"Here's the section number for books." The librarian hands me a slip. Does a stud like that hurt? "You can also check the Internet and the holdings of other libraries on the combined catalog. We can have books sent from any library in the state."

"Thanks."

I search the library, but Lucia's not here. I sit down at a table and begin looking at books. "The crossing between Africa and the Americas was called the Middle Passage. Over four centuries, millions of Africans were captured and shipped to North America, South America, and the Caribbean. Exact numbers are not known, but estimates are that thirty to sixty million Africans were taken from their homeland. As many as twenty to forty million people died on the way to ships or crossing the ocean. Only one-third, approximately ten to twenty million, reached the New World."

Thirty to sixty million people taken as slaves is so overwhelming that it's impossible for me to get my mind around the number. But then I read something very specific. "So many people died and were thrown overboard that schools of sharks followed the ships. If the Atlantic Ocean were drained, there would be trails of bones indicating the major routes of the Middle Passage." Why haven't we learned this before?

Walking back from the library I decide four things:

One, I need to know more about things like the Middle Passage.

Two, I'm sick of Dad running my life.

Three, I'm not asking anyone else to homecoming.

Four, I've always done things with Zach, but I'm not sure about steroids.

■■   ■■   ■■   At home, Mom's gardening in the front yard. "Look, Miles, the monarchs love the meadow blazing star."

"Yeah." Orange butterflies flit among purple spikes.

"Monarchs winter in Mexico," Mom says. "They look fragile, but they're resilient. They'll be back next year."

"Yeah."

"Grandma called. She's eager to see us next week." Mom weeds around the blazing star.

"Yeah."

"What's the matter with you?" She stands up.

"Why's Dad got to be like that, always blowing up?" The words burst out. "Why do we have to walk on eggshells trying to be perfect, trying not to make him angry?"

"Listen, Miles. Quit feeling sorry for yourself. You're not the only one with problems." Mom pulls off her gloves. "Your dad hasn't had it easy. Don't forget, he lost his mom when he was thirteen, and those boys had to look out for themselves." She shakes her gloves at me. "Your dad's father was difficult, very difficult."

"But why's he always on me?"

"He wants you to do better. He doesn't want you to make the same mistakes he did." Mom sits down on the front steps. "Your dad cares deeply, Miles. He loves you."

"Well, why doesn't he show it?"

"He shows it in lots of ways. He always has. I remember in the delivery room when you were born. He was so excited. 'Look at the size of this guy,' he told the nurses. 'He's going to play football.' The hours playing catch with you. Coming to your games. Your dad supports you in lots of ways. It's not his way, though, to talk about how he feels. You have to accept that."

"Why?"

"Because that's the way he is."

■ ■ ■ On Tuesday, Fox is running first offense and Coach Stahl is clapping. "Let's go, men. Crisp blocks. Drive them. Look sharp."

Jonesy in his sling and Stillwell on his crutches stand by the bleachers. Fox floats a pass that begs to be picked off, and Jonesy shakes his head. It's a huge drop-off at quarterback.

On defense, we run drills, but the energy level is low. Everybody's still in shock after losing two quarterbacks in two weeks.

"We'll end with special teams. Punting team, line up," Coach Stahl shouts. "Go live."

We haven't hit in practice since Jonesy got hurt, so I'm ready to crack someone.

"We've made some changes," Stahl says. "Defense, go all out to block the punt."

Zach jogs back to receive. Brooksy spots to prevent a fake, and I line up at right end.

"Down, set, hit," Adams calls.

I charge out of my stance and cut the corner. Nobody blocks me, and I've got a wide-open shot. I dive and feel the solid thump of the ball on my arm.

"Good block, Man," Zach cheers.

"You're holding the ball too long, Adams," Stahl says. "Punt the damn thing. Do it again."

"Down, set, hit."

I rush off the line, and again nobody touches me. I dive and block it a second time.

"Dammit, Adams. Quit jacking off." Stahl smacks him on the helmet with his clipboard. "Speed it up, or we'll get a new punter."

When the offense comes to the line, Tyson points at me. "Don't block it." Should I let up? Stahl said to go all out.

"Down, set, hit." The count is quick, and I'm a half second slow. I cut right behind Tyson, dive, and get my fingertips on the ball. Third block in a row.

"What the hell's the matter with you?" Stahl yells. "You can't get a punt off?"

Normally everybody's excited about a block, but nobody's enjoying this.

"Manning, where are you coming from?" Stahl barks.

"End of the line," I say. "Nobody's blocking me."

"I didn't ask you about being blocked," Stahl shouts. "Do it again."

Now I don't know what to do. If I go hard and block it, Stahl will explode. If I let up, I'm not showing how easy the punt is to block.

"Down, set, hit." I'm going after it. I run hard, dive, and feel the thump on my arm. I got it again. Adams gives me a look of sheer hate.

"You guys disgust me," Stahl says. "We're going to run this until you get it right. I don't care if we stay out here all night."

"Coach, I think if the end took one step back that would provide enough —"

"I don't care what you think." Stahl yanks my face-mask. His onion breath is overpowering. "Let's get one thing clear, Manning. This isn't a democracy. This is a dictatorship, and I'm the dick." He lets go of my helmet. "Open your mouth again and you're on the bench Friday."

Stahl's out of line. Sepolski's in charge, not him. "Do it again," Stahl yells.

"Let him get it off so we can go in," Tyson growls. I ease up and let Adams punt.

"That's the way, Adams." Stahl claps his hands. "See, Manning, it didn't have anything to do with the blocking. Let's run it one more time and then we're done."

Should I block it to shove it in Stahl's face or let it go?

"Down, set, hit." I slow down to let Adams punt.

"That's it, men." Stahl claps his hands. "That's better."

Sepolski stands on the far sideline with his arms crossed. He hasn't said much all practice. Stahl's run everything.

Stahl blows his whistle. "Men, Coach Sepolski has something important to tell you."

We all walk over and kneel down in front of Sepolski. His face looks pale. "Uhhh, ummmm." Sepolski clears his throat and rubs his head. "You guys have been a fine group to coach."

Have been? I didn't hear right.

"You know how much I love football, how much it means to me." Sepolski's voice is softer than usual. "But there are some things more important. One of these is health. I found out I've got prostate cancer. My doctor wants to do surgery right away to keep it from spreading."

What?

"He says I can beat it, but he wants me to make some changes. He insists I cut down on my stress. He wants me to step down from coaching this season. I don't want to do it, but I'm going to follow his advice."

I can't believe it. It's one thing to lose players, but Coach *is* Confluence football. I can't imagine another coach. I can't imagine playing for someone else.

"I love working with you guys. It's the best thing I do." Sepolski rubs his hand across his eyes. "I will miss it more than you can imagine. But right now, I've got to beat this."

I feel numb. Coach is the one who made me a starter. He's the one who encouraged me to play hard, play smart, have fun.

"For the rest of the season," Sepolski says, "Coach Stahl will be in charge."

chapter fourteen

■ ■ ■ Nobody says anything in the shower. I turn the water on hot and it blasts my back. I fold my arms on my chest and stare at the pool of water in the bend of my arm.

First Jonesy, then Stillwell, now Coach. Bad news comes in threes, but this is terrible. I don't want to think about Stahl being head coach. I soap myself and piss. It's a small release after all the bad news.

"C'mon, Miles." Zach is dressed. "Let's go."

In the truck we ride in silence. Finally, Zach says, "Coach Stahl's a good coach. He's got a lot of energy, new ideas. We can use that."

"I don't know. I've got a bad feeling."

"What kind of attitude is that?" Zach swerves to avoid a dead squirrel. "Coach Stahl deserves a chance. Give him a break."

"Why can't he give me a break?"

"Listen to what he says. And don't talk back." Zach turns up the CD. "You taking those pills?"

"Yeah." Why am I lying to Zach? He wants me to be a better football player. So does Dad. They have different ways. I've got to find my own.

"Tyson's ordering some new stuff, better gear," Zach says. "We'll get it this week."

I don't know what I'm doing. I don't like lying to Zach.

■ ■ ■ September's garden time at our house. At dinner we have corn, eggplant, zucchini, basil, potatoes, cucumbers, and tomatoes that Dad grew. The only thing not from his garden is the bread, and if I mention that, he'll probably start growing wheat and make me grind the flour.

"I've got some bad news." I set my fork down.

"What?" Martha says. "You're not going to the dance?"

"No, it's *real* bad." Mom looks worried. "Coach Sepolski has cancer. He's going to have surgery. He's stepping down as coach."

"What kind of cancer?" Mom asks.

"Prostate."

"What's prostate?" Martha looks to Mom.

"Part of the male reproductive system," Mom says. "Did they catch it early?"

"I'm not sure. Coach says he's going to beat it."

"Who's the new coach?" Dad stops buttering his corn.

"Coach Stahl."

"He's been waiting for his shot." Dad frowns. "But this is a bad time to take over."

A week ago Dad was all over Sepolski, but he doesn't

look pleased now. "Coach Stahl's walking into a tough situation," he says. "Make sure you listen to him. Make sure you respect him."

My stomach twists in knots and I can't eat. I'm sick of bad news.

▌▌ ▌▌ ▌▌ After dinner, Martha invites us to the front lawn for a science demonstration. "You fill a bucket with water and swing it around in a circle, and even when it's upside down, not a drop spills. That's because of centrifugal force."

"Centrifugal force," Mom says. "That's impressive."

Martha fills an ice-cream bucket three-quarters full and starts spinning it like a human windmill. She's right; not a drop spills out.

"Brava!" Mom claps.

"Cool trick." I pat Martha on the head.

"What did you think, honey?" Mom asks Dad.

"Big buildup for such a simple demonstration." Martha's smile disappears. "But it's good. Good science."

The Villareals, neighbors from down the street, ride by on their bikes. They wave and we wave back. I try to imagine what we look like — a happy family together on the lawn. What a small part of what happens in a family other people see.

▌▌ ▌▌ ▌▌ I'm floating like a bird, gliding above trees along the river. I can tell from the land that I'm above Confluence, but there are no buildings or people. I glide past the spot the rivers come together and continue north along the Clearwater. Then I realize I'm flying. I panic. How am I going to stay up? How do I avoid crashing? I drop lower. Trees come closer, darker, full of sharp branches.

My arms flap faster and faster. That doesn't help. I'm plunging down. There's nothing to cushion my fall.

Suddenly I jerk awake. I'm shaking. A dream, just a dream, but the images are so clear. I go to the bathroom and look in the mirror. My eyes are bright and wide, as if I've seen something bad.

Back in bed, I can't sleep. I roll and turn, and each time I close my eyes, I see green shapes with white dots shifting and spreading. They look like cells under a microscope and then form a word in block letters: CANCER. Coach Sepolski said he's going to beat it. As if cancer were our next opponent. As if he can call new plays, make the right adjustments, and score more points.

"Our Father, who art in heaven." I pray for Coach, who's been like a father to us. The repetition helps ease my anxiety.

Then I remember Stahl's head coach. That's a real nightmare.

chapter fifteen

▌▌ ▌▌ ▌▌ On Wednesday, there's a note on the locker-room door: FOOTBALL PLAYERS — REPORT TO THE GYM IMMEDIATELY!

"File in, men. Take a seat on the bleachers." Coach Stahl wears a gray shirt marked HEAD COACH. Behind him is a huge blue sign: SECOND PLACE IS FIRST LOSER.

"I don't want any of you thinking about second place." Stahl points to the sign.

I'm confused. I haven't been thinking about second place. I've had other things on my mind, like Coach Sepolski having cancer.

"Second place . . ." Stahl holds the pause for emphasis. ". . . is first loser. We're not in the business of being first losers."

What's he on? We're not in business. We're in school. Then I remember Dad's warning about respecting Stahl.

"Men." Stahl scans the bleachers looking at each of us. "You are about to begin the most important six weeks of your lives."

I watch faces. Zach's listening closely. So are most of the guys. I hope this isn't the most important six weeks of my life.

"That's right, men." I can tell already how much Stahl likes calling us men. "Because the next six weeks will determine whether you're champions or first losers. Think about it, men. You decide."

I bite the inside of my cheek. Coach Sepolski never talked to us like this. Stahl paces with his hands behind his back like he's a general addressing soldiers. "That's right, men. It's up to you. Let's see a show of hands: How many of you think of yourselves as first losers?"

I'm tempted to raise my hand. After Kyra Richman, I've got as much reason as anyone.

"Now, who wants to be a champion?"

Everybody raises their hands. Some of the sophomores raise two, but that's not enough for Stahl.

"I asked you a question. I want an answer. Who wants to be a champion?"

"I do," some of the linemen bellow.

"I can't hear you. Who wants to be a champion?"

"I do," everybody yells. Everybody but me.

❚❚ ❚❚ ❚❚ At practice, everything's different. "We're going to play power football, smashmouth football. You need to be in shape for that. Let's have fifty sprints." With Sepolski we used to do ten. "Don't give up. Don't give up." Stahl looks at me. I keep my head down and run.

We do endless laps of "darkness." Every time Stahl blows the whistle, we fall to the ground, do a push-up, and jump back up. He blows the whistle again and again. "I have a high tolerance for other people's pain," he yells. "You need to be bigger, stronger, faster. You've got two choices: Become men or quit."

I'm totally wrung out. I'm bending over with my hands on my knees. Zach's grinning. He's holding up better than anybody. I just want to make it without puking.

"One hundred push-ups," Stahl shouts. "Make sure your chest touches the ground." Coach Sepolski seems light-years away. This is Stahl's team now.

"Starting tomorrow, I want everybody in the weight room an hour before school four days a week," Stahl says. "I'll post a schedule with stations and reps. We'll see who's serious. It's simple. If you don't lift, you won't play."

I know I should lift more, but weight lifting doesn't determine how hard you hit or how smart you play. It doesn't matter what I think, though. There's one way now: Stahl's way.

■ ■ ■ Later, when we break into first defense, Coach Stahl comes down to talk to us. "Men, there are two types of football players," he says. "Thinking players and reacting players."

Stahl points to his head. "Thinking players observe, analyze, and make correct decisions. These are the players best suited for offense."

What's his point?

"Reacting players don't think; they react. A play happens. Boom. They're on it. These are the players best suited for defense."

Thinking and reacting aren't separate. You need to do both in football.

"Now, men, as defensive players, you react. When you see movement, you pursue. You're lions ready to kill. Don't think. React."

This is stupid. Dad always says good players are smart players.

"The coaches will prepare the defense. React properly, and you will be champions. React poorly, you'll be first losers." He looks at me. "Is that clear?"

Of course not. How do you *not* think? But nobody, including me, has the guts to say it.

■■ ■■ ■■ I go to the library because the book I requested is in. *The Middle Passage: White Ships, Black Cargo* has a picture on the cover of black men with ropes around their necks being guarded by a white soldier. In the distance, a ship waits to take them across the ocean.

I sit down in a chair by the window and open the book. After the introductions, it's all black-and-white illustrations, one horrible picture after another. The ghostly image of a sailor rips a mother away from her child. Rats gnaw on the bodies of slaves in chains. A diagram of a tightly packed slave ship is imposed on a black man's body.

But the most disturbing picture is one of people jumping overboard to kill themselves. Sharks swirl around the bodies, and at the bottom of the ocean is a trail of skeletons. I can't get this image out of my mind, and rather than take notes, I stare out the window and imagine the horror.

chapter sixteen

▮▮ ▮▮ ▮▮   "Pain is weakness leaving the body." Stahl's pacing around the weight room. He's wearing shorts and a blue muscle shirt with B T T R in huge letters.

I'm finishing ten reps of 110 pounds on the bench. Lifting first thing in the morning isn't my idea of fun.

"Push it, Manning. Push it." I strain on the last lift. "You've got to do better than that," Stahl says. "We need strong corners."

On the next bench, Zach whips off twelve reps of 150. Do the steroids make it that easy? Would I be lifting like that if I were taking them? "That's the way, Zach." Stahl claps. "Lookin' good."

When we finish, Stahl hands out muscle shirts. "B T T R, men, stands for 'better than the rest.' You've made a commitment to football, a commitment to weight lifting, a commitment to excellence. You are superior to other students. You bleed and sweat for the glory of the school. You are better than the rest."

I can't believe he's saying this.

"Wear these shirts with pride. You know what B T T R means, but don't tell other kids. They wouldn't understand." Stahl chomps his gum. "Men, you are members of an elite fraternity. Head off to first period."

Last year, I remember how proud I felt when I wore my varsity jersey. Everybody in school could see that I was on the team. Now, after chanting yesterday and B T T R today, I feel like I'm in some kind of cult.

In Halloran's class, kids scramble to staple papers. Strangler claims he didn't finish because he had to take his ferret to the vet.

"Your ferret wasn't sick because he ate your homework?" Halloran asks.

"Not the final paper," Strangler says. "He ate the rough draft, and he's allergic to ink. That's why I had to take him in."

"Bring it in tomorrow," Halloran says. "I'll take points off for being late, but if you write a story about your ink-eating ferret, I'll add a few back." Halloran collects papers. "What was the most shocking thing about the Middle Passage?" he asks.

"How long slavery lasted," says Strangler. "Africans were taken as slaves for over four hundred years."

Halloran nods. He seems surprised Strangler knows this.

"How strong people had to be to survive the journey."

"How many Africans died."

"How the ships were packed so tightly because they knew many people would die."

"How Africans were treated worse than animals."

"How much money was made in England, Holland, and Spain and how the American economy was built on slave labor."

"Yeah, slaves helped build the Capitol," Strangler says.

All kinds of kids are raising their hands, including some who usually don't. Halloran doesn't comment. He keeps calling on people.

"Lucia."

"I'm shocked by how religion was used to justify slavery. Many people believed it was God's will."

"Anybody else?"

I raise my hand. "I'm shocked that people dove off the ships to commit suicide rather than be slaves."

"Yes," Halloran says. "All these things are shocking. It's difficult to imagine, but I want you to try. Close your eyes."

I shift in my seat. Everybody closes their eyes.

"Let's explore this," Halloran says. "Imagine if someone showed up in Confluence, put a gun to your head, and locked you in chains. Imagine being dragged from your family, held in prison, packed in a boat. Imagine being beaten by people who spoke a language you didn't understand."

I try to picture this.

"Now imagine what you would have done if you had the chance. Would you have jumped overboard to kill yourself or would you have tried to survive?"

My mind blanks. I don't know.

"Which action do you think was braver?"

I don't know that either.

■■ ■■ ■■ At lunch on Friday, guys are talking loudly at the football table. Fox already looks nervous. What's he going to be like tonight with blitzing safeties and trash-talking linebackers?

"You'll do fine, Foxy." I slap him on the shoulder. He doesn't look convinced.

Zach waves me over. Am I imagining it, or is he getting bigger? "Shipment's in."

At his locker, Zach looks both ways, then opens the door. On the middle shelf are three bottles and three syringes. "This is the best way to juice," he says. "Meet me and Tyson here after school."

I glance at the syringes. This is moving too fast for me. "I don't know."

"What do you mean?"

"I'm not sure." I've never liked needles, but I can't tell Zach that. "I looked up some side effects: liver damage, acne, shrinking testicles, impotence."

"You scared?" Zach closes the locker as a group of band students comes down the hall.

"I'm not scared. I just don't know if it's worth it."

"Of course it is. You need some guts. You need to be willing to pay the price." He slams his hand on the locker, turns his back, and stalks off.

Roid rage. That's another side effect. Guys going off. Zach didn't used to blow up like that.

■■ ■■ ■■ I've got half an hour after school before the bus for Twin Falls. I'm not as fired up as I was last week. Maybe because Fox is the quarterback. Maybe because Stahl is the coach. Maybe because I'm not down with Zach and Tyson shooting up.

At my locker, I move my Spanish book from the middle shelf to the lower one. Sometimes I play these games, as if changing which shelf a book's on will improve my luck. Lots of athletes are superstitious, whether it's what they wear, how they get dressed, or who they stand next to. I carry this into my school life, too.

When the books are right, I close my locker. Coming down the hall carrying a violin case is Lucia. Light reflects off the blue beads of her necklace. She's seriously pretty.

Zach would know what to do. He'd say something smooth. I freeze. The only thing I can think of is, "Hi."

"Hi." She keeps walking.

I turn to watch. I wouldn't have a chance with her. She takes long strides away from me. Say something. Talk to her.

"Lucia," I call.

"Yes?" She turns around.

"I'm Miles Manning."

"Hi." She comes closer. I wipe my sweaty palms on my pants. She's wearing jeans and a tight T-shirt that says: Save the Drama, Call Your Mama. I don't know what that means, but I like it.

"I heard you were at the library Saturday."

She squints.

"The librarian said someone tall with dark hair and green eyes had been in." I can't believe I'm talking about the library. "I thought it must be you."

"Yes, I was there." She sounds puzzled.

"How do you like Confluence?" Why am I so nervous? Why am I talking like an idiot?

"It's okay, but I miss my friends. I miss the city."

"Yeah." My mind races for what to say. Lucia seems so calm standing there. She's got beautiful eyes and long lashes. "Are you going to the football game tonight?"

"No, I go to my dad's on the weekend." She checks her watch. "I've got to get going."

"Have fun." I try not to sound disappointed that she's not here on weekends. I open my locker and pretend to get a book so I can watch her. She moves gracefully down the hall, like a dancer.

"Lucia," I call.

She turns. "Yes?"

"What's your last name?"

"Lombrico."

Lucia Lombrico. I like that name. "See you Monday."

"Yeah, see you."

Sometimes, moving a book for good luck works.

chapter seventeen

■■ ■■ ■■ In the locker room at Twin Falls, Zach puts on pads next to Tyson. I choose an empty spot on the other side of the room. Sam Hunter is bent over with his pants stretched out on the floor.

"What the hell are you doing, Hunter?" Tyson asks.

"Putting both legs on at the same time. If their coach says, 'Those guys put their pants on the same way we do,' I want him to be wrong."

Tyson shakes his head. "You're one weird mother."

"Thanks, Ty." Sam slides his pants past his knees, both legs together.

Coach Stahl enters. "Attitude plus aptitude equals altitude. Think about it, men. If you have the right attitude and the right aptitude, which is another name for skills, you can go as high as you want. Attitude plus aptitude equals altitude." Stahl rubs his mustache.

That must have taken him ages to think up.

"Some of you need to work on your attitude." He looks at me. "Some of you need to work on your skills, your aptitude. But when you put them together, we can conquer the mountain that is the state championship."

Where does he get this stuff?

Stahl climbs onto a bench. "You know what you need to do. Just win, Eagles. Just win. We've got two victories. At the end of this game, I want three. Three and zero and we're on track to be . . ."

Stahl rips down a piece of paper exposing the word CHAMPIONS. "What do you want to be, men?"

"Champions."

"What?"

"Champions!"

"What? I can't hear you."

"CHAMPIONS!"

Stahl jumps off the bench and leads us onto the field. Sepolski used to shake our hands, then walk out behind us. I miss him more than ever.

❚❚   ❚❚   ❚❚ In the first half, both defenses shine and both offenses struggle. Coach Stahl is protecting Fox by calling running plays. Twin Falls knows this, so they're stacking nine guys on the line, daring us to throw.

On defense, we've shut them down and quieted the crowd. They've been three plays and out on every possession, and we've given the offense good field position. Fox hasn't done anything with it.

In the locker room at halftime, Coach Stahl sends the Gatorade jug flying. "This town is the scum of the earth.

These guys are the scum of the earth, and you're tied with them," he shouts. "What does that make you? Scum of the earth."

Sweat drips off my face. I wipe it with a towel as Stahl barks at the defense. "If the other team doesn't score, we can't lose. It's that simple. Hold them to zero. Anything more, you give them a chance."

I'm stunned. Rather than tell us we're playing well, Stahl's raising the standard to perfection. What about the offense? What's he going to tell them? That no matter what they do, it's still the fault of the defense if we lose.

"I don't care how bad you hurt. I don't care what's the matter with you. Go out and rip the heart out of them," Stahl's yelling. "Leave everything on the field."

I look down at the diamond pattern on the floor. Did the men who built this room ever think it would be the site of such stupid speeches?

"Hold them to zero, men, and we won't lose. What are we holding them to?"

"Zero," guys shout.

"What?"

"Zero!"

"What? I can't hear you."

"ZERO."

I'm sick of this rah-rah crap.

■■ ■■ ■■ Halfway through the third quarter, our punting team runs onto the field. Twin Falls loads two guys on the end. They're going for the block.

"Down, set, hit." Number 31 runs in untouched. He stretches out and blocks the punt. The ball bounces right to a teammate who grabs it and runs in for a touchdown. The crowd bursts into cheers. Just like in practice. Nobody blocked the end. Extra point is good, too. It's 7–0. Defense hasn't given up a point and we're still behind. Our special teams suck.

Stahl throws his headset down and screams, "Adams, you're done. Monson, you're the new punter."

In the fourth quarter, Twin Falls plays conservatively, protecting the lead. On third and three, their pulling guard leads a sweep my way. I race up to fill the gap. I remember Dad saying, "Go low. Go underneath him." I hit the guard at the ankles and come up underneath. I put my helmet into the ball carrier and rip at his arms.

"Fumble." Krause picks up the ball. Tyson flattens the quarterback. I cut the running back at the ankles. Somebody grabs Krause's jersey, but he shakes loose. He cuts back and zigzags into the end zone. Touchdown.

"We're back in this." Brooksy slaps my helmet.

I smack my fist into my palm as I run to the sideline. Dad stands along the fence clapping. I'm glad he saw that.

"Way to go, Man," Jonesy yells. "We needed the D to score."

"Tie game," Stahl shouts. "Hold 'em again, defense."

"Watch it deep," Jonesy warns. We're playing three-deep zone, so my responsibility is the right third of the field. I check the wind. The flag hangs limp on the pole.

Three downs gain four yards, and Twin Falls prepares to punt. I line up outside.

"Hut one. Hut two." I rush off the line and try to slide past the blocker. He stays with me, though, and the punt booms off. Zach makes a fair catch at our forty-one.

"C'mon, offense, one score," I holler as we run to the sideline.

Two running plays get nothing, so Coach Stahl calls a pass. This is risky.

"Down, set, hit." Fox drops back and watches Brooksy all the way. Fox lofts a pass to the sideline, and the defender steps in front for the interception. Luckily, he slips and his knee hits the ground. Otherwise, he had clear sailing for a touchdown.

It's 7–7. We've got to hold them.

With 1:53 left, Twin Falls faces a third and five from our thirty-two. Tie game. I slide over to cover the wideout.

Sometimes in football a play unfolds that is so well designed, so beautiful in its execution, that it will haunt you forever.

"Hut one." The quarterback drops back. The receiver comes at me and hooks in. The quarterback pump fakes, but I don't bite. I stay tight on my guy as he cuts for the post. Out of the corner of my eye, I see the tailback running for the sideline. Where's he going? The quarterback looks downfield for the bomb, so I stay with my guy.

Suddenly the quarterback turns and throws a bullet to the sideline. Who's there? The tailback has cut upfield. *It's a brilliant play* flashes through my mind as I rush to cover. I leap, but the ball sails over my outstretched hand into the arms of the tailback. He coasts across the goal line. My guy. Touchdown Twin Falls. The crowd erupts in cheers. I want to disappear.

"Where the hell were you?" Stahl shouts.

"I thought —"

"That's exactly your problem." Stahl's red with rage. "You thought. You thought. How many times do I have to tell you? React. You didn't react and they scored."

I replay the touchdown in my mind as our offense runs one bad play after another. I should have left the first receiver earlier. I should have protected my zone. I should have raced to the side as soon as I saw the tailback. I should have reacted better. I should have jumped higher. I should have tipped the ball away.

0:06. 0:05. 0:04. The seconds tick down, and I feel helpless.

0:02. 0:01. 0:00. Final score: 14–7. I got burned. I cost us the game. Everyone in the stadium saw.

Everyone, including Dad.

chapter eighteen

▮▮ ▮▮ ▮▮ The locker room is as quiet as the middle of Greenland. Losing always hurts, but this one rips me up. I turn the shower handle to red and hot water pounds my neck. There's no way to wash away the pain of a loss like this.

I was so conscious of the wideout going deep that I stayed with him. During the play, I thought I heard someone yelling, "Tailback, tailback," but it didn't come from the Confluence bench.

I go over the play again and again. Touchdown Twin Falls: 14–7. The result's always the same. I feel frozen in place as I stare at a clump of hair on the drain.

"One play, Man. One game," Brooksy says. "Let it go."

I appreciate that, but I've never been good at letting things go. I replay it over and over. Across the room Zach whispers to Tyson. He doesn't look my way.

Coach Stahl begins his pacing. "We lost the game. We didn't play aggressive football. We didn't react." I bend my head because he's looking at me. "Still we were right in it until the end. Then one play cost us. Some guys got cocky. They thought they were smarter than the coaches. They thought they'd do things their own way."

I look straight at him. This is so unfair I want to see his face. Now it's Stahl who looks away.

II   II   II I don't want to see anybody when we get back to Confluence, so I cross the parking lot to the Little League field and sit on the bleachers in the dark.

Zach and I played Little League here. That's when we became best friends. I played second base, and he was shortstop. One game we were way ahead, and it was threatening to rain. Mr. Barlet wanted to get the innings in to make the game official. He had Zach and me bat left-handed so we'd make outs. Zach smacked a shot to right. I looped a hit down the left field line, and Zach raced to third. We looked at each other and couldn't stop laughing.

I cross the diamond to the football practice field. I remember watching high school players when I was in grade school. I thought they were huge. I thought they were adults. Now that I'm in high school, I don't feel huge and I don't feel like an adult.

Last year when Zach and I made varsity, I thought we were set. I thought we'd start for three years and win a ton of games together. Now we're dressing on opposite sides of the locker room. Zach's hanging with Tyson, and he hasn't talked to me since I said no to shooting steroids.

As I walk down the street, I pass a house where a couple watches TV. The score of a football game doesn't change what they do. But losing the game feels like it's changed everything. We're no longer undefeated. We won't be conference champs. And Zach's not there for me.

II   II   II   Brick steps drop down to a tree that hangs over the river. I climb out on the trunk and watch the dark water below. It wouldn't be difficult to drop in. How fast is the current? How far would it carry me? How long would it be before anyone realized I was gone?

I see the image of Africans diving off the slave ship. I wouldn't be able to do that. I'd try to survive. That's how I am.

I watch a branch float away, just like our undefeated season. Twin Falls isn't that good. If we lost to them, how are we going to beat anybody?

The water laps and splashes. It flows downriver whether anyone watches or not. Springs, swamps, streams, creeks feed small rivers that flow to bigger rivers on their way to the sea.

Still, I wish I hadn't given up that damn touchdown.

II   II   II   When I get home, Mom and Dad are watching *The Godfather*.

"Where have you been?" Mom pauses the DVD.

"Down by the river. Thinking."

"Thinking about how you got suckered on that touch-down?" Dad asks.

"Yeah."

"What did I tell you about getting too far over? Didn't you see the tailback? Who the hell did you think was covering him?"

"I stayed with the wideout too long."

"You've got to pass him off once another receiver enters your zone." Dad demonstrates with his hands. "You can't leave half the field open, especially when the quarterback has all day to throw."

"I know."

"Are you hungry, Miles?" Mom asks. "There's some chocolate cake."

"No, thanks."

"And what happened on that blocked punt?" Dad asks. "Who's got the guy on the end?"

"Coach Stahl says no one needs to block him. He says Adams is too slow."

"Well, Adams is slow, but you can't let someone rush in untouched."

"I know."

"Someone's got to put a shoulder on that guy to slow

him down. That doesn't make any sense, leaving your punter vulnerable."

I'm glad he's criticizing this rather than me.

"Protecting the punter is one of the simplest things in the game. You form a wall." Dad demonstrates the wall with his arms. "You hold your block. You run downfield. But you sure as hell don't let guys run in untouched."

This is Dad's way of not blaming me entirely for the loss. I appreciate it, but I can't think of anything else to say. "Okay. I'm going to bed."

"Good night, Miles." Mom turns the movie back on.

II II II In bed, when I close my eyes, I keep seeing the play. Someone's hollering, "Tailback, tailback." This time I recognize the voice. It's Dad. He's trying to warn me.

I replay coming up on the sweep and causing the fumble, but that's pushed away by the play I got burned on. Why is the mistake so much clearer? Why does that come in slow motion with all its detail?

One more image appears, Lucia. I should have told her I'm glad she's in Halloran's class. I should have told her I'm glad she's in our school. I should have said I liked her T-shirt. I hardly know her, but she's the one person I'd like to talk to after costing us the game.

chapter nineteen

■■ ■■ ■■ My first thought Saturday morning is that the game's a bad dream, another nightmare. The soreness in my back and arms, though, reminds me it's real. We lost. My fault. I can tell the pain of losing is going to last much longer than the aches in my body.

Downstairs, Martha's at the computer designing stationery. "Good morning, Miles."

"Morning." I don't want to think about the game, so I avoid the paper. Instead, I read the back of the Frosted Flakes box. Some lame idea about cutting out a circle to make a flying disc. Most people would go get a Frisbee. You'd have to be bored out of your mind to do the things on the backs of cereal boxes.

"Miles, how come you're not going to the dance?" Martha sits down.

"It's stupid. Everybody spends a lot of money to stand around and pretend to be grown-up. The whole thing's a joke."

"No, it's not. It's romantic. Kelsey's sister Maddie got a long teal dress, and she let us watch her try it on. She's going to The Landing for dinner, and she's wearing her hair up. She'll be beautiful."

"Great." I put two waffles in the toaster.

"You should go, Miles."

"Martha, I'm not going." I raise my voice. "I asked a girl. She said no. I'm not going."

"She said no? What's the matter with her?"

"She's already going with someone else."

Martha's eyes widen.

"It's okay. Besides, there's a new girl I kind of like." Why am I telling Martha about Lucia?

"Who is it? Who is it?" Martha bounces up and down.

"I'm not telling. But if anything happens, I'll let you know."

▌▌ ▌▌ ▌▌ After last night's game, I want to be by myself. The library's a good choice. Nobody from the team will be there. Nobody who wants to talk football. Nobody who'll remind me of the loss.

I find a copy of *USA Today*. There's a picture of kids in a limousine and an article about high school dances. Some guys spend thousands of dollars on limos, tuxes, dinners, and hotel rooms. That's beyond me. I couldn't do that on my Easy Rest money.

I look at the previews for the new TV shows for teen- agers. These high school kids look like models, are loaded with money, and have lots of sex. That's not my high school life.

The game keeps coming back. That same play. Twin Falls touchdown. I wish I could have it back. If I could erase those ten seconds, my life would be a lot better.

I don't want to read. I don't want to look at magazines. I don't want to go online. I'm afraid somebody will see me here and say something about last night. A few people look at me funny, like they know I lost the game for Confluence.

Walking home, my shoe sticks each time I step. A big wad of gum. Why can't people put gum in the trash? What do they think will happen if they throw it on the ground?

I sit on the curb and pick at the gum with a paper clip. It's deep in the grooves of my shoe and won't come off. I step in some sand to stop the stickiness.

■ ■ ■ Sunday after church, we go to Grandma's for brunch, like we do each month. The drive past corn and soybean fields feels far from the game. A man with a beat-up truck sells squash, melons, and pumpkins by the side of the road. Sumac in the ditch is changing green to red. I keep thinking about the loss. We'll drop out of the top ten.

Grandma's waiting on the porch. She comes down the steps smiling. "Hi, Miles. I got the picture of you from the paper. Congratulations." She gives me a hug.

"Thanks, Grandma."

"Boy, those roads were slippery," Dad says. "The ditch was full of cars." He thinks Grandma worries too much, so he always does this.

"The roads were bad?" Grandma looks confused.

"No, they were fine." Mom glares at Dad but doesn't say anything. She never does.

"Grandma, I can swing a bucket of water without spilling a drop," Martha says. "I can do it in the living room."

"No, no," Grandma says. "Not in the house."

"That bucket could come loose," Dad says, "smash a window, and send glass flying. People could get killed." He walks over to the TV and turns on the pregame.

I don't feel like football, so I sit on the porch with Grandma and Mom. They both are tall and thin and cross their legs the same. They push up their glasses the same way, too.

"Miles, how's school?" Grandma asks.

"Good." I don't want to talk about the loss.

Martha swings her bucket out front.

"Be careful," Grandma says. "I don't want anyone getting hurt."

Instead I sit in my chair and dread the clock counting down. Waiting is torture. Each second is one moment closer to everybody seeing the play that cost us the game.

Stahl runs my good play once and focuses on the fumble recovery. "Krause, heads-up play to find the ball. Tyson, solid block." He doesn't even mention that I caused the fumble.

I examine the concrete walls and exposed vents. There's not much to look at here other than the tape, and that's the last thing I want to watch. The game runs quietly, with no crowd noise, only Stahl's comments.

On the touchdown I gave up, Stahl runs the play over and over. He doesn't mention Keller, the safety, being slow to pick up the receiver. He doesn't mention the defensive line getting no pressure on the quarterback. Instead, it's all on me.

"Dammit, Manning. Look at that wide-open zone. You didn't react. We can't have that." He pauses the tape.

I nod my head. I don't need to look. The play's burned into my brain.

For brunch Grandma's made bacon, sausage, French toast, and scrambled eggs. "Our furnace has been making strange noises," Dad says. "I hope it doesn't blow up while we're gone." Everybody pretends to ignore him. He's not funny. Why doesn't Mom tell him to knock it off?

After brunch while I'm drying dishes, I notice the picture of a dark-haired baby in the corner of the dining room. I've seen it before but have forgotten his name. "Who's that, Grandma?" I set the serving plate on the shelf.

"That's James. He died when he was two, right before your mom was born."

"How'd he die?"

"Meningitis." Grandma says this calmly. "I also had another son who died. He was born prematurely. That was Daniel. He came right after Drew."

Two children who died. I wipe the bowl that's already dry. That must have been hard for Grandma.

In the living room, Dad turns up the volume on the game.

▮▮ ▮▮ ▮▮ Sunday night is film night, and after Friday's loss I don't want to go. Maybe I could call in sick. Maybe I could say we didn't get back from Grandma's. Maybe one of those disasters Dad made up struck.

1

▌▌ ▌▌ ▌▌ Monday, I leave Halloran's class at the same time as Lucia. "How was your weekend?"

"Okay," she says. "I heard the game didn't go well."

"Worse than that." I follow her, even though I usually go the other way.

"What happened?"

"I got burned and cost us the game." I feel lighter after telling her, like I've made a confession.

"I'm sorry." She looks at me with her green eyes and seems sympathetic. "I thought football was a team game." She stops at her locker.

"It is, but sometimes you're out there on your own. If you make a mistake, everybody sees it."

"Yeah." She gets a physics book. She must be smart. "What do you have second period?" she asks.

"Consumer ed." That doesn't sound so smart.

"I'm going upstairs. See you later, Miles."

I like the way she added *Miles* to that. I let that echo in my head as I run to class.

▌▌ ▌▌ ▌▌ At practice, Coach Norlander pulls me aside. "Coach Stahl wants to play some new guys," Norlander says in his high voice. "Keaton will practice at right corner with the starters. You need to switch jerseys."

What? I can't believe it. I look at Stahl, who's watching. "Tell Coach Stahl I'm surprised he didn't have the guts to tell me." I spit out my mouth guard, unsnap my helmet, and walk to the sideline. Sometimes a major change happens in such a simple way that you can't believe it. I'm not a starter. I've been starting since fourth grade. How can I not start?

Keaton hands me his white jersey. "Coach Norlander told me to switch with you."

"Screw him."

"Coach Stahl said —"

"Screw him, too."

"Manning, Keaton, hurry up," Stahl shouts.

I peel off my blue 42 like a layer of skin. Keaton grabs it and rushes to join the starters.

I throw his white jersey on the ground. I don't want a second-string jersey. Stahl didn't have the guts to tell me. The bastard.

"Four-three, cover one, man-to-man," Zach yells to Keaton. Why's he helping him? I take my helmet off and set it on the ground.

What do I need to do to get my spot back? Stahl talks about bigger, stronger, faster. Keaton's a hard-core weight lifter. Is he on steroids, too? Is that what I've got to do?

"One-handed sideline catches, men." Sam Hunter passes to a sophomore who tries to drag his toes like the pros.

"Out-of-bounds. Both feet weren't down," Sam says.

"Yes, they were."

"You were bobbling it. You didn't have possession when your toes were in." Sam sees me watching. "Manning, you want to try?"

"No, I want to get back in." I don't feel like part of the team standing here.

"Might be a long wait. It's boring watching." Sam motions for me to join.

"No. I want my spot back." I leave the white jersey on the ground and turn to the starters. Maybe Keaton will get hurt.

❙❙ ❙❙ ❙❙ Mom's getting ready for aerobics class when I get home. I pick up a rubber band from the counter and wrap it around my wrist. "Bad news."

"What?" She looks up from tying her shoes.

"I'm not starting. I lost my spot."

"Oh, Miles, I'm sorry. Maybe it's temporary. Maybe you'll get it right back." Mom doesn't understand football.

"I don't think so. Coach wants to try some new players. Guys who are good weight lifters."

"What?"

"Coach Stahl likes guys who lift all the time."

"Well, just do your best. Maybe Coach Stahl will change his mind. I know you feel bad, but don't get down on yourself." She checks the clock. "I'm late. Be back in an hour." She gives me a hug.

I snap the rubber band on my wrist. The person I'm not looking forward to telling is Dad. He's out in his garden digging rutabagas. I stand on the porch watching him set them in a burlap bag. I've got to tell him. I might as well do it now.

"I'm not starting."

"What?" His mouth drops in disbelief.

"I'm not starting. Coach Stahl had Keaton take my blue jersey."

"What did Stahl say?" He stabs the garden fork in the dirt.

"Nothing. He had Coach Norlander tell me."

"That gutless coward. He's less on the ball than I thought. Did he make other changes?"

"Adams isn't punting."

"So you and Adams are the scapegoats." He shakes his head. "Stahl's coaching scared. When that starts, things go downhill fast." Dad points his finger at me. "Do what's necessary to get your starting spot back."

"Okay." I could get up early and be the first one at

weight lifting. I could work harder and do more reps than anyone. I've still got that packet of D-Bol in my drawer. I could put on five pounds of muscle. That would show Stahl I was serious.

I'm sure Dad doesn't mean steroids, though. Guys didn't do that when he played. But he doesn't realize that our two best players, Tyson and Zach, are shooting up. Dad's got no idea how much high school's changed.

■■ ■■ ■■ "Write this down," Halloran says at the end of class. "Remember when we talked about your ancestors coming to this country? This is an extension of that. For Monday, talk with your parents, talk with your relatives, and build a family tree."

"That's a lot of work," Strangler complains.

"Be as specific as possible. Birth dates, marriage dates, death dates. At a minimum, three generations — you, your parents, your grandparents. Some of you will be able to go further. The more you do, the more credit you get."

After class, I see Lucia bending down at her locker putting papers in a folder. She adjusts the strap on her black bra. She looks good. "Do you know the information for your family tree?"

"Some of it." She puts the folder away. "After the divorce, some branches are broken." She says this softly.

I hadn't thought of that. How do you draw branches after a divorce? "Well, my mom had two brothers die," I say. "That's a type of broken branch."

"Really?" Lucia turns. "You must wonder what your uncles would have been like."

"Yeah." Though that's not something I've thought about.

"That must have been difficult for your mother."

"Yeah." That's not something I've thought about either. But if Lucia wants me to, I'll think about anything she suggests.

chapter twenty-one

❙❙ ❙❙ ❙❙ I stare out my bedroom window thinking about Lucia. What's she doing right now? Is she in her bedroom thinking of me? If I'm thinking of her and she's thinking of me, would we sense it? Would a feeling come over us at the same time?

I like talking with her, but I get so nervous. My mind darts around and she seems so calm. I jump from one topic to the next, rushing to fill the silence. She's such an interesting mix. She's shy and confident at the same time. Does she have a boyfriend at her old school, someone she sees on weekends? Probably. I don't think she'd go out with me.

Talking with Lucia about broken branches, though, felt different, like we had things in common. I don't usually talk about family stuff, but it felt natural with her.

Outside my window, the branches of the maple tree are bare. When the tree had leaves, most of the branches were hidden. Now it's bare branches until spring, when leaves appear and new branches on top start growing. Our family trees are the opposite, with the old ancestors on top and the new branches at the bottom.

Squirrels scramble in the yard collecting acorns beneath the oaks. People don't gather acorns, but they gather nuts from other trees, like pecans. Who was the first person to make a pecan pie? How'd they think of that when everybody else was using apples or cherries? And why is it only pecan pie? I've never heard about walnut pie or cashew pie. Those would be good, too, wouldn't they? Maybe I should invent a recipe for walnut pie.

But being an inventor is a difficult job. If I were captured by aliens and taken to another planet to demonstrate our technology, I'd be worthless. I couldn't explain how a computer or a cell phone works. I couldn't explain something as simple as a zipper. It has two sets of teeth, but I don't know how you get them to close. A zipper is actually quite amazing.

Sometimes when I'm thinking about something like zippers, I wonder why and try to retrace my path. Zippers came from inventors, but how did I get to inventors? Oh yeah, walnut pie. Walnuts came from trees, which came from branches, which leads me back to Lucia.

I don't know if other people do this, and I'm not sure why I like it so much. Maybe because it's mine. It's my mind, and sometimes I like to watch it wander.

"Miles, time to eat." Martha knocks on my door.

I still think walnut pie would be good, especially if it had that sweet goo pecan pie has.

"What were you doing?" Martha asks.

"Thinking about walnut pie."

"You're weird."

■■ ■■ ■■ I've been reading Dad's moods for years, so when he sits down, I can tell he's angry. These are the times when it's best to lie low. Even Martha is quiet.

"Pass the carrots to your father, Miles," Mom says.

Dad takes a bite of chicken and spits it out. "This is cold. How long has it been sitting around?"

"I can put it in the microwave for you," Mom says.

"I hate microwave chicken. I'll eat it cold like I do most nights."

We all know anybody who challenges him will get ripped to shreds, so we eat in silence. Dinner in our house is so often a disaster. Maybe we should call it quits and eat separately.

Finally, Martha tries. "This squash is delicious, Daddy."

"Emmm," Dad grunts. It's harder for him to get angry at her.

"What's bothering you, dear?" Mom asks.

"I'll tell you what's bothering me." Dad sets his fork down. "The gasket plant is shutting down for two months. 'Excess inventory,' they say. Management's been on them to increase production, and now they say they've got too much. How many guys do you think are going to buy paint when they're not getting paid?"

"Maybe some of them will do some painting with their time off," Mom says. "We'll manage for a couple of months."

"A couple of months." Dad slams his fist and the glasses shake. "I'm not worried about two months. Don't you see? This is what they want to do permanently. Shut down the plant. Send the jobs to China. What do you think is going to happen to this town if they close that plant? What do you think are the chances of a downtown paint store surviving?"

Mom doesn't answer and Dad raises his voice.

"I found out I need eighteen hundred bucks for the transmission because somebody doesn't know how to use a clutch." He looks at Mom. She tried to teach me to use the stick shift on his car. I lurched around a few times before deciding that automatic was fine.

"And Miles has college coming up in a couple of years." He turns to me. "I thought last year when you started as a sophomore, you might have a shot at a football scholarship. That would have helped. Now you don't even play. They don't give scholarships to people who sit on the bench."

Let it go. Let it go. Let it go, I repeat to myself. I want to scream.

"There are other scholarships besides football," Mom says. "Maybe Miles could get an academic scholarship."

"Academic scholarship? What makes you think those are easy to get? You have to be smart, not just a smart-ass."

"Michael," Mom says sharply.

Martha's bent over her plate crying.

"What are you crying about?" he shouts.

"I can't stand this."

"Then leave. Go to your room."

Martha rushes away crying louder.

"I've had enough." My plate's full, but I'm finished.

"Good. Get the hell out of here."

❚❚ ❚❚ ❚❚ Martha's facedown on her bed. "Here, take a Kleenex." I hand her the box.

"I don't know why he's like that." She sits up and blows her nose.

"I don't either." I pat Martha's back as she lies down and squeezes her stuffed duck.

Downstairs Mom and Dad argue about money. I bite the nail on my left thumb. It's already short, but there's a piece sticking up. I bite it, peel it, and feel pain. I shouldn't have done that, but the blood gives me something else to focus on.

Not starting is bad enough without Dad bringing up a scholarship. If football is so important to him, what do I count for if I'm not playing? If I'm not playing, why should I stay on the team? Maybe I should quit.

This used to be my room. There's a rough spot on the wall from the last time Dad hit me. He didn't hit me often, but I was so scared when he did. I must have been about eight, Martha's age. I can't even remember what I did wrong. I was lying on my bed and he stormed in. I was terrified. He swung his hand to hit me, and I pulled my knee back so hard that it hit the Sheetrock and went right through the wall. "You damn baby," he hollered. "You screamed before you got hit."

That hole reminded me of my fear. Dad didn't fix it for six months. I don't know why. Maybe it was a warning. I remember lying in bed, staring into that hole at the empty space between studs.

Dad and Mom are still arguing. What if they got divorced? What would it be like if he weren't here? Quieter. I try to imagine Dad living someplace else. How often would I see him?

"I hate it. I hate it. I hate it," Martha says.

I rub her head. "I know. I do, too."

chapter twenty-two

❚❚ ❚❚ ❚❚ "First defense at this end. First offense down there," Stahl shouts. All the starters in their blue jerseys run to their positions. I walk to the sideline with the guys in white. Football used to be a chance to forget bad things at home. Now, it's bad here, too.

Keaton's at right corner. He makes mistakes, but Stahl keeps clapping. "Let's go, men. Gotta react." How many mistakes does Keaton get? How bad does he have to screw up before I get my spot back?

Sam Hunter has a group around him. "Today's topic is electricity." He jerks his body like he's electrocuted. "Generate some puns we can plug into."

"Yeah, keep them current."

"Even if you're dim."

"There aren't many outlets for this type of humor."

"I'm amped."

"I'm burnt out."

"You're not burnt out. You're AC/DC."

I can't believe how fast these guys toss them out. Hunter sees me watching. "C'mon, Manning. Get grounded."

I look back at the coaches. "What does Stahl say?"

"We're scrubs. He doesn't care. If they need a second string to beat up, he'll yell for us."

I join the group and try to think of something about a lightbulb. "Manning, you're on," Sam says.

"Watt?"

"What?" Sam looks confused.

"Watt?" Everybody gets it now. Some guys groan.

"Live wire." Sam smiles.

"Second-string defense," Coach Norlander calls. "We need eleven guys."

Sam, me, and nine other guys rush onto the field. The goofing around is a way to pass time. Like me, these guys want to play.

"Twenty plays live." Norlander scratches his butt. "Don't hit the quarterback. Everybody else, full contact."

Sam is organizing guys into positions. "Miles, you've got your corner."

"Yeah." I run to my spot. It's a cool day with no wind, perfect to smash somebody.

"Ten plays. Straight up," Norlander squeaks. "After that, you can mix in a few blitzes."

Fox brings the offense to the line. "Down, set." He's sounding more confident. "Hit." He hands off to Monson on a dive. Sam, who's playing middle linebacker, grabs him and I plow my aggression into the pile.

"Three yards. Too much," Sam says in the huddle. "Let's see if we can shut these guys down. Ready?"

"Break," everybody hollers.

"Down, set, hit, hit." The defense flies to the ball on a sweep. Bunkers, the wideout, moves the other way.

"Reverse." I race to the line. Sam's pushed Bunkers so deep that by the time we pile on him, Coach Norlander is blowing his whistle.

"Twelve-yard loss." Sam is clapping. "Good call, Man."

This is what I've missed. Being with the guys, smashing the running back, stopping the offense from gaining a yard.

"Ten plays, the offense has nine yards. Throw in the twelve-yard loss and we're plus three," Sam says in the huddle. "Four-three, cover two. Now we can blitz. Miles, come off the edge."

Fox looks over the line and I move off the receiver and act casual. Sam jumps back and forth like he's blitzing, so Fox concentrates on him. "Down, set, hit." Fox tries a hard count to flush us out, but I stay back. "Hit."

I burst forward. Nobody picks me up. I'm in Fox's face before he sets to throw.

"Don't hit the quarterback." Norlander's waving his hands over his head like he's drowning. "Monson, you've got to pick up the blitz."

Sam's even more excited. "Beautiful, Man, beautiful. The timing, the angle, the color." Sam makes it sound like a painting.

"Watt?" I say, and he starts laughing.

"Huddle up," Sam calls. "Four-three, cover one. Play this straight. They're looking for a blitz. Watch the screen or the draw."

Sam's got good football smarts. Why isn't he starting? He's thinking about what the offense will do. He's making adjustments. Maybe that's his problem. Maybe he's thinking too much. Maybe Stahl doesn't consider him a reactor.

"Down, set, hit." Monson takes the draw, but nobody's fooled. Sam and the linemen shut it down for no gain.

"One more play," Norlander yells. "Everybody go all out."

"Norlander's setting us up." Sam's thinking out loud in the huddle. "Watch the reverse. Watch the bomb. Play it straight. Five-three, cover three. Ready?"

"Break." We've been flying around hammering everything. I love this game. I'm not quitting. I'm not giving Stahl that satisfaction.

Over by the soccer field, someone with dark hair and a purple fleece is leaning against the fence. Looks like Lucia, but she wouldn't be out here.

"Down, set, hit." Brooksy races off the line, pauses on a hitch, and takes off for the post. I'm on him like a shadow. I've seen this play before. I look back and Monson's sprinting to the sideline.

"Middle, middle," I yell to the safety and race toward Monson. Fox spins to throw. I leap for the ball, pick it off, and race the other way.

"Pick," Sam shouts. "Block somebody." He smashes into Tyson and they sprawl on the grass.

I run hard up the sideline behind other blocks. One guy to beat. Fox. I fake inside and he pauses. I break back outside and shove a stiff arm into his neck. He reaches for me but can't hold on.

I run all the way to first defense so Stahl sees. He ducks down pretending he's diagramming a play. I hold the ball over my head while Sam and the guys go nuts.

"Second defense outscores first offense," Sam shouts loud enough for Stahl to hear. "Manning's the Man."

One play to lessen the sting of that touchdown back in Twin Falls. As I jog back, I look over at the fence again. No one's there. Am I starting to imagine her?

∎ ∎ ∎   Wednesday night, I get out my family tree pages. I start with the information Drew gave me and organize the branches. I draw lines to connect people, but I don't have all the names and dates. I remember to leave room for Mom's two brothers who died.

What's Lucia doing right now? Sometimes I imagine there's a movie of my life. How would what I'm doing look? What if Lucia were watching?

I need to call Drew for help. "Hi, Stephen. Is Drew there?"

"This is Drew. Hello, Miles." I screwed it up again. "Good to hear from you." He's not mad that I haven't called, like I said I would. "I see on the Internet that the team's having troubles."

"Yeah, and I lost my starting spot."

"What happened?"

I tell Drew the story. He listens and says, "That doesn't sound fair."

It's not and that's what I want to hear.

"I've been watching quite a lot of football myself," Drew says. "Stephen's a Patriots fan and he gets tickets through work. We've been to every home game. I'm learning the language. Blitz. Stunt. Trap. Crackback."

"You got it, Drew." I pace around the porch as we talk. "Drew, I need to build a family tree for history class. Can you help?"

"Sure, Miles. I've got one up on my Web site. All the information is there for our side of the family."

"Excellent. My teacher wants us to include birth and death dates. Are those listed?"

"Yes, for everybody," Drew says.

"Including your brothers?" I think about the boys who would now be my uncles.

"Yes, they're part of the family."

"I'm sorry they died." I'm surprised to hear myself say this.

"I'm sorry, too." Drew's voice gets softer. "I think it affected all of us."

"I'll call again, Drew, not just when I need help with homework."

"Do that, Miles. One more thing, talk with your mom. She has some information that you need."

"Okay, Drew." I'm confused as I hang up. I thought Drew said all the information was there. Why do I need to talk to Mom?

▌▌ ▌▌ ▌▌ Twenty-three is my favorite number. I've always liked it, but last year when I chose it as my football number, I began to *be* 23. It isn't a double number, like 33 or 44, which are so popular. It's not divisible like 24 or 32. It's prime.

Once I became 23, I noticed the number more. I got my first interception at Deer Rapids on the twenty-three-yard line. I got 23 out of 25 on my algebra quiz three times in a row. I started setting my alarm for 6:23. Waking to 23 made it easier to start the day.

Often, when 23 is present, things go well. When 23 isn't there, things go bad. In August on jersey day, I was set for 23. Starters choose first, but when my turn came, Coach Stahl said, "There's no 23. You have to pick another number."

"Who got 23?"

"Nobody. We didn't get a 23 this year."

Coach Sepolski should have made sure we got 23. That's my number. That's me.

"You have to pick another number, Manning."

No other number comes close to 23.

"How about 24?" Stahl asked.

That's even and divisible by a ton of numbers. "No, not 24."

"Pick something then. You're holding up the line."

"How about 29?"

"No 29, either. Here's 42. We have to keep moving."

I examined 42. It's divisible by 1, 2, 3, 6, 7, 14, 21, and 42. It's an even number. The 4 feels too straight and rigid. After everybody finished, I went back. "Coach, I don't think 42 is right. Are there any numbers left?"

"Only this." Stahl held up 94.

A lineman's number. That's worse. "I'll stay with 42."

Some people don't believe certain numbers are better than others. Some people think the whole idea of having a favorite number is weird. But football players know there's a right number for them.

I tried to get used to 42, to adjust to it. But when Coach Stahl told me there was no 23, I should have known that was a sign of how things were going to go this season.

❚❚ ❚❚ ❚❚ Lucia's kneeling at her locker, and I'm excited to see her.

"Hey, Lucia, how you doing?"

"Good, Miles." She's rolling a purple mat and stuffing it inside a black mesh bag.

"What's that?" I try to sound relaxed.

"My yoga mat. I take a class through Community Ed."

"What do you do?"

"Basic poses, balance, flexibility, strength. It might help with football. You should try it."

"Maybe." I'd like to watch Lucia stretch, but I can't imagine myself standing on one leg in a yoga class.

I want to ask her if she was watching practice, but I'll be embarrassed if she wasn't. I need to know, though. "Were you at football yesterday?"

"Yes. I wanted to see." She pulls her hair back and wraps a turquoise band around it. I like it when she does that. She looks good in that black sweater.

"What did you think?"

"It's hard to tell who's who with those pads and helmets."

"Could you figure out who I was?" I kneel down beside her.

"Yes. They kept calling you Man. That's short for Manning?"

"Yeah." I'm glad she noticed.

"I like that." Lucia stuffs her English book in her backpack.

"I like the name Lucia. I like how it slides out of the mouth, Loosha."

She smiles. "It means 'light' in Italian."

"That's cool. Does Lombrico mean anything?"

Lucia scrunches up her face. "It means 'earthworm.'"

"Even *earthworm* sounds good in Italian."

"You think so?" She closes her locker.

"Lombrico, Lombrico, Lombrico. Sounds great."

Lucia laughs. "I saw you intercept that pass and run all the way down the field. I could see your joy."

Joy. That's a word coaches never use. That's exactly the feeling I had. Joy. "I'm glad you saw it."

"Then I got self-conscious," she says. "Nobody else was watching." Lucia stands, so I do, too.

I take a piece of paper and a pen from my pack. My mind's jumping. "Lucia, what's your phone number?"

Her cell phone ends in 23. That's a very good sign. At her dad's, the number ends in 5, which is 2 plus 3, and at her mom's the first digit is a 2 and the last is a 3. She's giving me all her numbers. She must want me to call.

"Those are good numbers."

"You're into numbers?" Lucia slings her pack over one shoulder and lifts her violin and the bag with her yoga mat over the other.

"Yeah, certain ones I like a lot."

"You're different, Miles." Those green eyes dance and I wait for more. "I like that."

▌▌ ▌▌ ▌▌ Watching a football game on the sideline in the rain is a drag. Keaton's playing okay, but I'd do better. I hope he screws up or gets injured. Nothing broken, just enough so he'd have to come out. I know that's not right, but I wish I was out there. I'd sure be warmer than I am standing here.

In the fourth quarter, with the game tied 7–7, a Downsville receiver catches the ball in front of our bench. Keaton dives for his legs. The receiver skips over him and runs into the end zone.

"What kind of tackle is that?" Stahl shouts. "A cheerleader could do better. Keaton, go to the bench."

I snap my chin strap to go in.

"Baker, get in for Keaton on the extra point."

I'm stunned. Baker's a sophomore who's never played varsity. I can't believe it. It doesn't matter what I do; Stahl's not going to play me. The rain falls harder.

It's third and seven at the Downsville twenty with 1:13 on the clock. Fox hands off to Monson, who follows Tyson. Downsville defenders slip and slide, but Monson churns ahead.

"Dig, Monson," Zach hollers.

Tyson rumbles downfield and flattens two guys with one block. Monson splashes into the end zone. Touchdown.

It's 14–13. We're down by one. Stahl calls Fox over.

What would Sepolski do? He'd kick the extra point for the tie and go to overtime.

"Go for two for the win." Stahl taps Fox on the butt. "Run the reverse pass." What kind of play is that to run in the rain?

"Down, set, hit." Fox hands to Monson on a sweep. Downsville defenders pursue. Monson hands to Brooksy on a reverse. Brooksy runs left, but defenders close in. He slips, regains his balance, and flips a pass to the end zone. Fox is wide open and makes the catch. The referee raises his hands. Confluence wins: 15–14. The few people who are left in the stands scream and hug each other under their umbrellas.

Guys swarm the field and tackle Fox and Brooksy. Zach points at me. "Gutsy call by Coach Stahl. I told you he could coach."

I'm glad we won, but I didn't contribute anything. My jersey's clean. No dirt. No blood. No grass stains. As if I weren't here. As if I weren't on the team. I stand off to the side watching everybody else congratulate the stars.

chapter twenty-four

■ ■ ■ "You ever been shining?" Sam asks after the game.

"What's shining?"

"You starters with your single-minded worship at the altar of football have no idea how many aspects of the full high school experience you're missing. C'mon, we'll introduce you to the wide world of shining."

I don't feel like going to Izzy's after not playing, so I'm happy to be invited. At Taco King, we meet Toilet and Cooper. Toilet's real name is Jeremy Bohl, but he's been called Toilet forever. Both he and Cooper start on the soccer team. They both call Sam "Gatherer" rather than "Hunter."

"Can you run?" Cooper looks me over.

"Yeah, sure."

"You know those football players," Toilet says. "They like a rest every play."

After Jumbo Burritos, we drive south in Sam's van to Oxbow Lake. "The two elements in a successful shining operation are surprise and creativity," Sam says. "Come to think of it, those are two essential elements in most things." Sam's drumming on the steering wheel as he talks. "I've got an idea for a double barricade, but first we need to show Miles a basic procedure. Let's call it Shining 101."

Sam knows the park like his own backyard. He points to a car at the end of the road. "Parker on the overlook."

Sam pulls the van behind some trees. "Here's a flashlight, Miles. We'll sneak up. When Toilet gives the signal, shine your light on the happy couple. No telling what you'll see."

I can't believe they're doing this — that I'm doing this. Because the leaves are wet, it's easy to stay quiet as we move from tree to tree. When Toilet waves his arm, we jump out and shine our lights. A couple break their embrace in the backseat and blink at the lights. It's Troy Gratz and Claire Hudson. Troy reaches for his glasses and Claire buttons up her shirt. Troy's a puny junior in chorus. I've always thought Claire was hot. What's she doing with him?

"All clear, Throckmorton," Cooper says in a deep voice. "It's not your grandmother. Carry on, you two. Sorry for any inconvenience. We had reports Throckmorton's grandma was out here."

"This little light of mine, I'm gonna let it shine," Sam sings as we walk back to the van. I feel a mixture of embarrassment and excitement, like I'm playing a game and don't know the rules.

We pile into the van and Sam drives past the empty beach. "Double barricade time," he says. "Twice the fun." He slows on a hairpin curve. "Here's the first spot. Let's collect a bunch of stuff and set it beside the road."

The rain has stopped and it feels good to move after standing on the sideline. Toilet brings in an old section of wooden fence. Cooper rolls a cedar log. Sam's found two tires. I've got a couple of small branches.

"You've got to do better than that, Miles, my Man," Sam says. "We're building a barricade. Pretend it's the French Revolution."

I find a dead Christmas tree in the ditch and drag it back.

"That's better," Sam says.

We pile stuff behind lilac bushes at the side of the road.

"Hop in, men. We're going, men, to the lower spot, men. Nothing less, men, than total commitment, men. Don't be the seventeenth loser or the nineteenth loser. Remember, men, altitude plus bad food equals altitude sickness."

Toilet and Cooper look confused, but Sam's got Stahl's voice and gestures down. I'm laughing so hard, I'm afraid I'll piss my pants.

"Shining is for reactors, men. Brain surgery, men, is for thinkers." Sam taps his head. "If you're doing brain surgery, men, don't react. If you're shining, men, don't think." He claps his hands.

Cooper shakes his head. "Aren't you glad you don't play football, Toilet?"

Sam parks and we all gather more brush and branches. "Here's the plan," he says. "We'll make a wall of this stuff. A couple out for a drive will be shocked to see a barricade. They'll turn around, which will take a while because the road is so narrow. While they're doing that, we'll build another barricade back at the first spot. They'll be trapped."

"Good plan, Gatherer." Cooper starts pulling stuff, and we join in.

After the barricade stretches across the road, we go back to the first spot. We stand together and wait. The woods smell of pine and wet leaves. We hear a car.

"Showtime, boys," Sam says. "Make sure you're hidden."

I duck behind an old oak and feel the bark with my hands. A red Expedition drives by. "Perfect," Sam whispers.

We scramble to make the barricade. Past the curve, I hear the SUV turning around. All four of us lift the section of fence on the barricade, then duck behind trees.

The SUV comes around the curve, races up the hill, then slams on the brakes. Toilet and Cooper are already laughing.

"Lambert and Carlson," Sam whispers. "Beautiful."

Jason Lambert's a senior swimmer who's a complete jerk. Courtney Carlson's even worse. They both look scared.

"Ouuuuuuuuuuuu, ouuuuuuuuuuu." Toilet makes owl sounds.

"Caaaaaaaaaa, caaaaaaaaaa." Cooper's a crow.

Lambert panics and punches through the barricade on the side. Branches scratch against the side of the SUV as he gets hung up. He drives back, forward, back, forward, before he's free.

"Ayyyyeeeeeeeee, ayyyyyyyyeeeeeeeeeee."

"What's that?" I ask Sam.

"A hyena."

"Why would a hyena be out here?"

"That's what makes it so scary."

I can't help laughing.

"I'd love to be there," Sam says, "to hear Lambert tell Daddy why the Expedition's scratched up."

After hauling branches and running through the woods, I feel like I've had a workout, as if I played a game.

These guys are different. They're seniors, but they're not into partying and trying to be popular. They don't care about fitting in or what other people think. How different from Tyson's party two weeks ago.

Sam drops me off at my house. "Thanks, Sam. That was fun."

"Yeah, Beyond. That's a good initiation."

I don't get it until he's driven off. A new name. Miles Beyond. I like it.

▌▌ ▌▌ ▌▌ I get up at 11:30 Saturday morning. Downstairs, I find a note from Mom on the kitchen table:

> *Miles,*
>> *Martha's at Kelsey's. I'm going to the mall.*
> *I'll be back for lunch.*
>
>> > > *Mom*

I unwrap a breakfast bar and hear the mailbox slam. I go to check. Bills, credit cards, and a magazine in a brown cover. Addressed to me. What's this?

Inside, *Testosterone Extra* has a glossy close-up of a bicep: "GET THE MUSCLES CHICKS DIG." Where did this come from? Then I remember clicking that box for a trial issue.

One headline asks, "DO YOU WANT MUSCLES LIKE THE FINEST THOROUGHBRED?" The small print says a product developed for horses is now available to "hard-core athletes interested in peak performance." Developed for horses?

Another article describes turning steroid pellets into powder to prepare them for injection. "Pick up pellets dirt cheap at livestock stores." Some guys will do anything. The article also recommends drugs to get "hard wood" when you're experiencing "equipment failure" from taking steroids.

"Order Now — Risk Free." I don't think so. Taking drugs developed for horses or livestock isn't risk free. I bury the magazine deep in the trash. That's the last thing I want Mom finding. She'd totally freak.

I've still got those steroids from Zach. I hurry upstairs and take the packet from the drawer. I don't need these. I dump them in the toilet and flush. The pink pills whirl around the bowl. One bobs back up. I flush again and it disappears.

Mom's car pulls into the driveway. I check the toilet once more to make sure all the evidence is gone, then wash my hands.

"Miles, I'm back."

"Okay. Just a second."

I want to ask Mom about that information Drew mentioned. I pick up the family tree that I printed out from his

Web site. He's got names and dates for six generations. I'll get loads of credit for this.

In the kitchen, Mom slices an apple into quarters, then hands me two.

"Here's the family tree from Drew." I sit down next to her.

"That's great." Mom glances at the pages as she crunches her apple.

"Yeah, but Drew said you had some information that I need."

Mom takes off her glasses and rubs her eyes. She looks tired.

"What is it?"

"I don't know." Mom stares straight ahead, like she's seen a ghost. "I have to talk with your dad. I'm not sure."

That night my parents argue in the kitchen. I hear the rise and fall of voices, but not what they're saying. Then one word bursts clearly from Dad.

"Faggot."

chapter twenty-five

❙❙ ❙❙ ❙❙   Easy Rest Mattress, like me, is sleepy Sunday morning. I unlock the door, turn on the lights, and wake the store. I check the computer to see what Zach sold yesterday. No customers yet, so I can make some phone calls.

I dial Lucia's phone. No answer, but I like hearing her voice on the message. I try the number at her dad's.

"Hello," a man with a deep voice answers.

"Is Lucia there?"

"No, she's at yoga. Can I tell her who's calling?"

"Manning. Miles. No, Miles Manning. Please tell her I'll call back this afternoon."

"Okay, I'll give her the message."

Lucia's dad sounds nice. If someone messed up his name when he called our house, Dad would be all over him. "What? You don't know your own name? Call back when you figure out who you are."

The bell rings and an after-church couple comes in. The man is bald with a round face, and her face matches his. I explain the difference in firmness based on coil counts and layers in the mattress. They know they want something that will last a long time, so I sell them our top-of-the-line king-size set. Good way to start the day.

The man reminds me of someone else I need to call. I page through the book and find Joseph Sepolski. No "Coach," just Joseph Sepolski. That doesn't look right.

"Coach, this is Miles Manning."

"Hey, Miles." His voice sounds raspy.

"How are you doing, Coach?"

"All right. I'm off the smokes. The doctor likes that. They've got me on radiation treatments. Hormone therapy after that. Estrogen. I may start wearing a dress and high heels." Sepolski coughs. "How about you, Miles? How are you doing?"

"Okay," I lie.

Coach knows too much to let that slide. "How's it really going?"

"Coach Stahl's made changes. I'm not starting."

"I heard." Sepolski clears his throat. "You're a good football player, Miles. Be ready. You'll get another shot."

"Thanks, Coach." That's the kind of guy Sepolski is. I call him to see how he's doing, and he ends up making me feel better.

"We miss you, Coach."

"I miss you guys, too."

"Good luck with the treatment."

"Thanks, Miles."

▌▌ ▌▌ ▌▌ I check the production list to see what to make — an eighty-two queen mattress. I throw an innerspring on the table, pull a piece of Typar, and tuck it into the corners. *Chunnc, chunnc,* the hog ringer blasts staples that catch the coils. I add a foam topper, a cotton batt, and convoluted foam. I pull the cover over the top. *Chunnc,* the gun blasts a staple into the corner coil. Grab, hold, *chunnc,* grab, hold, *chunnc,* I work my way around what's beginning to look like a mattress. I flip it over to start on the other side.

If Sepolski were coach, I'd still be starting. Zach and I would be the corners. If Sepolski were coach, Zach might not have gone hard-core on steroids. Maybe Sepolski would have said something to make Zach think. Maybe not.

Chunnc. A searing pain shoots through my left finger. I lift my hand and the whole unit comes with it. I've stapled myself to the mattress.

Don't panic. I try to pull my finger away from the coil, but the pain is intense. The hog ring is locked tight. *Don't panic.*

Where's the wire cutter? I slide the mattress to the next table using my right arm. The wire cutter isn't on the tool bench. Who didn't put it back? Zach. I'll kill him. *Don't panic.*

Where the hell is the wire cutter? I slide the mattress back to the first table and lift up the foam. Pliers, but no wire cutter. *Don't panic.*

I bend down to see how the hog ring goes into my finger. Right through the tip with the staple wrapped tight to the coil. I twist the pliers. The pain shoots down my finger. Damn. I need a wire cutter. *Don't panic.*

What should I do? I can't stand here. I've got to get help. The phone's on the other side of the room, but I've got no choice. I slide the mattress off the table with my free arm and lean it onto the floor. The staple pulls against my skin. Slowly, I lift the mattress from the table and stand it on end.

I push the mattress along the concrete. That hurts. I kick the garbage can out of the way, so I can pull the mattress against the wall to reach the phone.

On the third ring, Dad answers, "Yeah."

"Dad, I've had an accident at work. I stapled my finger to a mattress."

"Well, unstaple it."

"I can't find a wire cutter. Can you bring one?"

"You should always know where your tools are," Dad says. "I'll be over."

I wish I hadn't had to call but feel relieved Dad's on his way. What if Mr. Hurst, the manager, shows up for one of his surprise visits? I'd be fired on the spot. The pain in my finger feels worse.

The front bell rings. That's too fast for Dad. A lady looks around. I wave and she waves back. I'm sure she wonders why I'm not coming out.

She waves again and I gesture for her to come back. She opens the door of the factory cautiously.

"I'm sorry. There's been an accident." I point to the coil. "I stapled myself to the mattress."

"Oh dear, you're being brave." She clasps her hands together.

Brave. Stupid is more like it. I reposition the mattress to take some pressure off my finger.

"How can I help?" she asks.

"You don't have a wire cutter, do you?"

She digs through her purse as if there's a chance. "Lots of junk in here," she says, "but no wire cutter."

"My dad's on his way. He'll bring one. Can you sit up front and tell anybody who comes in that the store's closed temporarily? Tell them to come back in half an hour."

"I'd be happy to do that."

Next time the doorbell rings, it's Dad. He says something to the lady and she laughs. Probably something about his son being a complete idiot.

Dad bursts through the factory door. "What did you do that for?" He examines my finger to see how it's attached to the coil.

"Sorry."

Dad positions his orange-handled wire cutter and makes one strong squeeze. My hand pops free. Two metal points stick out of my finger, but there's no blood. "You got a first-aid kit?"

"Yeah." I point to the blue box on the wall.

Dad takes out disinfectant, gauze, and a Band-Aid. "Let me see." He holds my finger in his hand and pulls the points out. He applies disinfectant and wraps a Band-Aid tightly.

"Thanks."

"You had a tetanus shot lately?" Dad hands me the points.

"Yeah, last year after I cut my arm at the barn."

"Okay. Get back to work. You better help that lady."

"I will. Thanks, Dad."

"One more tip. Watch what you're doing."

❚❚ ❚❚ ❚❚ Sunday night, I remember my homework for Halloran's class. I find Dad in the basement emptying the dehumidifier. "I've got a few questions for my family tree project." I take out my notebook.

149

"We're not like your mother's family. We don't call attention to ourselves by putting up a Web site for everyone in the world to see. We protect our privacy."

I hadn't asked about that. "Can we start with your grandparents?"

"I've got what you need in my head." Dad bends down to replace the container, and the dehumidifier hums on. He gives me the Irish names and dates for two generations. It's not as detailed as Drew's information, but it'll be fine for class.

"What about your immediate family?" The boxes at the bottom of my page are empty.

Dab rubs the stubble on his cheek. "My dad died when I was twenty-five. My mother died when I was thirteen." Dad says this in a matter-of-fact tone, as if he's repeating a script.

Thirteen. Three years younger than I am. Imagine if Mom died and left me and Martha with Dad. I remember Mom saying Dad's father was difficult. I'd like to ask Dad about this, but I don't think he'd want to talk about it. He slams an empty tube of caulk out of the gun.

"Anything else?" he asks.

"One last question, your brother?" I know Dad doesn't see him, and I can't remember meeting him.

"What about him?"

"His age? Where he lives?"

"Shawn's two years older than me. He was fifteen when Mom died. He and Dad had some major fights. Last I heard, he was down in Belize. Says he's a scuba instructor. That means he hangs out on the beach and smokes dope."

Dad grabs the gun and a new tube of caulk. "I've got to finish that shower."

"Thanks, Dad."

"Yup." He clomps up the steps.

Dad doesn't talk to his own brother, and both his parents are dead. Is that why he resents Mom's family? Is he jealous that she and Drew get along and that Mom still has a mother to talk to?

I feel my finger throbbing. I need more Tylenol.

Later, I think about Dad as I lie in bed. He's impossible to figure out. I wanted to ask him what he and Mom were arguing about last night. But he would have bitten my head off and told me to mind my own damn business.

Then I remember talking to Lucia's dad. I never called her back. What if she hung around waiting? How could I forget to call Lucia?

chapter twenty-six

❚❚   ❚❚   ❚❚   Blue and white homecoming signs decorate the school. Each one is a reminder. I don't start. I don't play. And I'm not going to the dance.

I try to catch Lucia's eye in Halloran's class, but she's talking with Dylan Hines. Dylan's the starting shooting guard on the basketball team, and he's smooth around girls.

"A family tree is another way to see who you are," Halloran says. "Pick a partner and discuss the branches of your family. Also, discuss how you see yourself in relationship to these branches. Are you more like your mother's side, your father's side, a blend of the two, or neither?"

Kids slide their chairs and I go to Lucia. "Can I be your partner?"

"Dylan already asked." Lucia turns her chair and I look at her back. I should have called her.

"Miles, do you have a partner?" Halloran asks.

"No."

"Charlie needs one."

Charlie Dunston hasn't finished his assignment. "I asked my mom and dad, but they both had to work last night," he says.

I show Charlie my family tree, but I'm concentrating on Lucia and Dylan. Already Lucia's laughing at his jokes. I tell Charlie I'm more like my mom's side. Most of the time.

At lunch I sit next to Strangler. He's not going to the dance either. "Let's do something fun," he says. "Anyway, who wants to dress up in a suit and stand around at a boring dance?"

"Lots of people," I say.

The cheerleaders have arranged all kinds of lame dress-up days for homecoming week: favorite TV character, punk rock, goofy hair, mismatch, and blue and white. The only activity that's worth anything is the burping contest. Jonesy cuts loose with superstar belches and wins in a landslide.

■■ ■■ ■■ I sit next to Sam in the locker room Friday. I've already participated in part of his pregame ritual — two Tostada Supremes at Taco King. "Gotta have fuel for listening to inspirational speeches," Sam says. From the smell, some of that fuel's turned to gas.

Zach's dressing next to Tyson across the room. Putting on pads knowing I'm not playing is like getting dressed for a party I'm not going to. When I was a starter, I reviewed my assignments and visualized playing well.

Now, Sam's pushing me to put on my pants two legs at a time.

"I don't want to. It doesn't make sense."

"Just like Coach's speeches. Put your pants on this way, you'll stay in sync. Try it."

I lay my pants on the floor and slide them up, both legs together.

"Perfecto," Sam says. On the other side of the room, Zach shakes his head.

During the game, cheerleaders yell behind us:

F, *clap, clap,* I, G, H, T.

F, *clap, clap,* I, G, H, T.

FIGHT, FIGHT, let's FIGHT.

Spelling is very important for a Confluence cheerleader.

Stahl paces the sideline in shorts, even though it's forty-five degrees. This shows how tough he is. "It's our homecoming, men. This is our house. Show Concord how we protect it."

The defense gets frustrated with the offense, and guys blame each other. Baker makes two bad plays in a row, but Stahl doesn't chew him out. Maybe he's got nobody to put in. Nobody but me.

"You should replace Candlestick Maker," Sam says.

"I know." I want to hit somebody.

Tyson throws an elbow pad down. "We're playing like a bunch of fags."

Would he talk that way if he had an uncle like Drew?

"We're better than this," Zach shouts. "Kick some ass."

We lose 24–6, but it doesn't feel that close. We're three and two. Hard to believe we started the season talking about going to State.

❚❚   ❚❚   ❚❚   The night of the dance, Strangler and I are bored out of our minds by 7:00.

"I've got an idea. Let's go shining."

"What's that?" Strangler sits up.

"Shining. You've never been shining?" I act like I'm an expert.

After finding flashlights at Strangler's house, we drive to Oxbow Lake. A full moon is up and it feels good to get out of town. I explain shining to Strangler as we drive through the park.

"There's a parker." We circle around, leave the car, and sneak through the woods.

We jump out and shine our lights. A couple with messed-up hair rises from the backseat and blinks at the light. They look like college students. She looks surprised, like she can't believe we're doing this. He looks angry.

"Run," I tell Strangler, but he's halfway down the road. He's in shape from getting ready for hoops. I chase after him.

It's strange doing this without Sam, Cooper, and Toilet. The jokes and songs were what made it fun. As we walk to the second spot, Strangler tells me about the basketball team.

"How's Dylan?"

"He looks good. He's going to have a big year."

That's not what I want to hear.

A pickup is parked at the overlook. Strangler and I duck behind some trees and get our flashlights ready. A pinecone crunches as we creep in front of the truck. As soon as we shine our lights, a door slams and a guy jumps out.

"Run."

We run down the road, but the guy's right behind. I cut into the woods, but he's fast. Branches crack as he chases me. *Run.* I duck under some pine boughs, but he's still coming. *Run.* I splash into a creek and up the other side. *Run.* I loop back to the beach, but he's still there. Maybe I should dive in and swim for the other side. It would be cold, but he wouldn't follow me.

Underneath a light pole, I'm jerked back by a pull on my collar. I stumble as fists hit my chest, stomach, and face. I put my hands up to protect myself, but the guy punches like a madman. "Okay, okay," I say.

"It's not okay. You — dirty — little —" He slugs me for each word.

"I've never done it before," I lie.

"You won't do it again." The guy's big and has a goatee. He holds his right fist in front of my face. The letters T I M E are tattooed on his fingers. He smells like he's been drinking. T I M E smashes into my face. My legs wobble, and I drop to my knees.

He lifts me up by my hair. "You've got someone to apologize to." He pushes me in the back, and I stagger along the road.

Where the hell is Strangler? Why didn't he help? I wipe my nose with my hand and see blood mixed with snot. What am I doing here? I should have asked someone else to the dance. That's where I should be, not in the park getting beat up.

A girl with long blond hair is sitting in the truck. She rubs her eyes like she's been crying. "This lowlife has something to tell you," Goatee says.

"I'm sorry."

"Sorry for what?" Goatee growls.

"Sorry for bothering you, for shining flashlights, for harassing you, for interrupting your evening." I try to think

157

of anything else I can apologize for. "I'm sorry for being such a loser."

"Tell your friend," Goatee says, "that if you two try that again, I'll beat you so badly, you'll piss blood." He drags me to the back of his truck and reaches in for some orange twine. He pulls my arms behind my back so hard they feel like they're popping. He ties them tightly and leads me to the rock ledge. "You're pathetic," he says, and pushes me off.

One thought flashes in my mind: *If I land on the rocks, I'm dead.* I look down and see black water. I arch my back to protect my face and go under. The water's cold and I can't see anything. I kick wildly. I need air.

I burst through the surface gasping for breath. My nose hurts when I breathe. I'm farther from shore than I expected. I lean forward but can't move. I flip onto my back and kick. It's slow going with my hands tied, and I'm shivering with each breath. I've got to get out. Kick harder.

On shore, I scramble onto the rocks. I slip and fall and rip my pants. I'm shaking. I've got to move to warm up. I run around the ledge to avoid Goatee. What hurts most: ribs, stomach, face, nose, hands, knee. No, what hurts most is that I let him beat me up. I didn't fight back.

Strangler's waiting at the car. "Where the hell were you?" I ask. "Untie my hands."

"I ran the other way." Strangler works on the knot while I shiver. "Hold still. I've almost got it."

■■ ■■ ■■ I've never broken my nose before, and getting it fixed is no fun. Gauze gets jammed up my nostrils; cartilage gets shoved and twisted. I can hardly breathe. Then the doctor says, "I've done the best I can, but I'm afraid your nose won't look exactly the same."

My nose wasn't that great before. Now I expect it will be a real beauty.

But all of this is minor compared with listening to Dad. "I don't know why the hell you were in that park at that hour. Strang never had any sense, but what were you doing? If you were sneaking up on guys and their girl-friends, you deserve a busted nose."

How does he know everything?

chapter twenty-seven

▮▮ ▮▮ ▮▮ I can't remember a morning when I wanted to go to school less. I've got a new zit on my chin, a broken nose, and two black eyes. The last thing I want to do is explain what happened.

"Raccoon," Jonesy calls as I walk into school. "Been out to Oxbow?" That damn Strang.

Other kids join in. "Lots of raccoons in the park."

"Be careful about shining them."

Walking to Halloran's class, I hear Sam singing "Rocky Raccoon" in a loud voice.

"Rocky." He puts his arm on my shoulder. "Lots to learn about shining. Full moon, clear night, not ideal for stealth. But those shiners. Beautiful."

"Yeah. Thanks."

"One other thing, Mr. Beyond. Some girls go for that raccoon look."

▮▮ ▮▮ ▮▮ At practice, I dress early and put my helmet on to hide my face. Coach Stahl gathers everybody at midfield. "At ease, men. Take off your helmets."

Just what I need, another speech.

"Wearing the blue and white is an honor." Stahl pats

his chest. "You need to treat the colors with respect. All the time, not just when you're wearing them. This weekend, some players disrespected the colors."

I concentrate on individual blades of grass. He can't be talking about me.

"Three players were at a party on Saturday night. Sheriff deputies found marijuana and methamphetamines." Stahl spits these syllables like they're poison. "The players claim they weren't using drugs. That's not good enough for Confluence football. They should not have been there. That's a violation of the Conduct Code. I have no choice but to suspend them for the rest of the season."

I look around. "Who's gone?"

"Three sophomores," Sam whispers. "What a joke."

Everybody knows Tyson and the linemen party every weekend. They laugh about it at practice on Mondays. But their parties never get busted. One rule for the stars. Another rule for the scrubs.

And Stahl keeps pushing weights. Isn't he curious how some guys lift more all of a sudden? Doesn't he wonder about guys bulking up quickly? Or is it easier to take the results and look the other way? "Just win, Eagles. Just win."

"Men, uphold the honor of the blue and white. We go to North Fork on Friday and we need 110 percent effort."

Stahl starts pacing. "Not 70, not 80, but 110 percent. Do you understand?"

"Yes, Coach," everybody shouts.

Everybody but me. If 100 percent is the max, how can you give more than that? If Coach says he wants 110 percent, why not 112 or 205 percent? If 100 percent isn't the max, what is? This is 100 percent bad math.

"Manning." I'm brought back with a jolt. "What happened to your face?"

"I got in a fight, Coach."

"Well, it doesn't look like you did much of the fighting." Zach and Tyson lead the laughter.

❚❚ ❚❚ ❚❚ Thursday evening I call Lucia. No answer. I dial the number at her mom's.

"Hello," a woman answers.

"Is Lucia there?"

"No, she's out."

"This is Miles Manning. Do you know when she'll be back?"

"She's at the library. I don't expect her back until 9:15."

"Thanks." I check how I look in the mirror. Horrible. What am I doing searching for Lucia looking like this? But I've got to talk to her. I comb my hair. Like that will take attention away from my black eyes. I grab my sweatshirt. I can always act like I'm there to check out a book.

Lucia's not in the magazine room. She's not at the computers on the second floor. Maybe she's not here. Maybe she lied to her mom. Maybe she's out with Dylan.

The librarian with the tongue stud is at the reference desk and I'm desperate for information. "Excuse me, have you seen a high school student with black curly hair and green eyes? Tall, a girl. I was supposed to meet her."

"You mean Lucia?"

"Yeah, Lucia."

"She's in the reading room downstairs. That's where she always works."

"Thanks."

Along the river are three rooms with big windows that face west. I didn't know they were here. In the last one, surrounded by books, is Lucia. She's wearing a big sweatshirt and is leaning back on a chair with her bare feet up. She looks good whatever she wears.

"Hey, Lucia."

"Hi."

"How're you doing?" I close the door behind me.

"Fine." She locks in on my eyes and nose. "How are *you*? I heard what happened."

"I'm okay."

"Does it hurt?"

"Nah." I want to change the subject. "What are you reading?"

"Some stuff on slavery." Lucia sets down a book on the Middle Passage.

"For extra credit?"

"No, for myself. I've been reading about slave ship crews. I wonder what my ancestors were doing. I wonder if any of them were slavers."

No one I know thinks like this. "So you come down here to read."

"Yeah, but sometimes I sit and stare out the window."

The pink sky reflects in the water. "Lucia, I'm sorry for not calling you back. I had an accident at work."

She pushes the sleeves of her sweatshirt up. A leather bracelet wraps around her wrist. Her arms are thin but strong. Is that from yoga?

"You've been having a lot of accidents lately."

"Yeah. I was hurrying to finish at work so I could call you."

"Really. Are you making that up, Mr. Manning?"

"No, not at all." I like the way she says "Mr. Manning." I like the way she's found this room overlooking the river for her own. But most of all, I like it when she tells me she's not going to her dad's this weekend because he's traveling.

"Do you want to go to a movie Saturday night?" I ask before I realize it.

"Sure. What's playing?" Lucia pushes a strand of hair behind her ear.

"I don't know." My mind's racing. She said yes. Lucia said yes. I hadn't thought to check what's showing. "I'll find out. Whatever, it'll be fun."

"I'd like that, Miles."

Lucia Lombrico said yes. Finally, I've got some news for Martha.

ll ll ll "Where have you been?" Dad's cutting up a chicken at the kitchen table when I walk in.

"The library."

"Did your mother know where you were?"

"No." I rub my hand over my nose. It still hurts.

"You're supposed to let her know." Dad's pissed about something. "What were you doing?"

"Homework."

"Homework? How do you do homework when your backpack's here?" Dad slices the leg from the body and pulls it apart.

"Some extra homework. I was looking up stuff." I hang up my sweatshirt. Why's he bent out of shape?

"With who?"

"A friend."

"Who?" The lines in Dad's face deepen when he's angry.

"Lucia Lombrico." I stand facing Dad.

"That figures. Instead of concentrating on school and football, you're running around, getting your nose busted, chasing girls. Ever since you lost your starting spot, things have gone to hell."

I bite my lip. I'm sick of these lectures. Between Dad and Stahl, I've been ripped repeatedly.

"You've been sticking your nose where it doesn't belong. That's why you got it busted." Dad points his knife. "And quit bothering your mother with questions. You've asked enough. And quit talking to that fruity brother of hers."

"Where's Mom now?"

"Upstairs, reading to Martha."

I haven't asked Mom anything more about the information Drew said I need.

"Can I ask you a question, Dad?" My hands are shaking and I take a deep breath.

"What?"

"You tell me to treat people with respect —"

"That's right," he interrupts.

"Then how come you don't treat Mom's family with respect?" My voice is clear. "You don't respect Drew. You don't respect Grandma."

Dad's eyes widen. "You don't know the half of it. I don't like people sticking their nose in my business. Those people are in-laws. That's what in-laws do, interfere."

"They're family." I look straight at him. "They deserve respect."

"Don't tell me how to treat anybody." Dad bangs the table with the knife handle. "Don't be shooting your mouth off when you don't know what you're talking about. You're the one who needs to show respect."

"I show respect." I point to myself.

"Not when you sneak off to meet some girl in secret."

"It wasn't secret. I'm sixteen. I can talk to who I want. I can make my own choices."

"You're living in my house. You follow my rules."

I walk out of the room and my hands are still shaking.

chapter twenty-eight

■■   ■■   ■■   Zach and Tyson are discussing the defense as I get on the bus to North Fork. At the start of the year, I sat with Zach. That seems so long ago. I look the other way to avoid eye contact. In the middle of the bus is Sam.

"Miles, those black eyes still looking sexy to the ladies?" Sam's got an empty seat next to him.

"Can I sit here?"

"I'd be honored, Mr. Beyond."

As we drive out of Confluence, hills shine with the red and gold of turning leaves. Black horses run across a field, and their muscles glisten. Farmers harvest corn on a perfect day to be in the fields.

"Look at all that food," Sam says. "Over 90 percent of the corn and beans going to fatten hogs and cattle. Sixteen pounds of grain to produce one pound of beef. If we ate more of it directly we'd have lots of food for hungry people. But we love our cheeseburgers."

Instead of discussing defensive assignments, we're talking about agriculture.

"Two more games," Sam says. "My high school career is almost over."

"What're you doing next year?" I scratch my finger-nail on the armrest.

"I applied early to Amherst."

"Where's that?"

"Western Massachusetts, in the Pioneer Valley. Beauti-ful campus, and get this: They want me to play football."

Sam doesn't even start in high school. How's he going to play in college?

He sees my surprise. "Oh, it's Division III. I stayed with a linebacker on my campus visit. I met the coach and some of the guys. They're cool. They have fun. Treat it as a break from studies."

"Wow." Sam will play next year. Some of the hard-core seniors might never play again in their lives.

"Big world out there, Miles. Confluence is a dot. What colleges are you thinking of?"

"Don't know. I haven't thought about it much."

"You've got time. Loads of good schools."

"I've got an uncle who lives in Massachusetts. Boston. I'd like to see him."

"Excellent," Sam says. "Amherst isn't that far from Boston. You could stay with me, too. Check out some schools."

"That'd be good." I could see Drew and Stephen without Dad. Then go see Sam.

The game's another blowout, 31–0. North Fork's good this year. We're not. Zach picks off another pass, though, which gives him five for the year.

Might as well give him his hundred bucks. That was a bad bet.

❙❙ ❙❙ ❙❙ I'm standing in the backyard with a rake on Saturday. Dad doesn't believe in leaf blowers. "They're too damn noisy," he says. "Besides, raking's good for you." I mound pile after pile of oak, maple, and catalpa leaves. As I'm stuffing the twentieth bag, Mom comes out.

"There's something I want to tell you." She's got her jacket zipped all the way up. I follow her to the bench under the twisted branches of the catalpa.

"When you were doing your family tree, I didn't answer honestly." Mom looks down and exhales a big breath. "I talked with your father. We agreed it was time to tell you." She takes off her glasses, rubs her eyes, then puts them back on. What's she trying to say?

"I got pregnant when I was eighteen," Mom says quietly. "Your father had come back from the navy on leave."

I can't believe this. Dad got Mom pregnant at eighteen.

"As soon as we found out, we decided to get married. My mom was angry. Drew was angry. My mom said some mean things to your dad." Mom opens her hand and spins her wedding ring on her finger.

"It was a hard pregnancy. Because it was my first, I didn't know what to expect. The baby was born prematurely and had problems with his lungs. He stayed at the hospital three weeks before coming home." I watch Mom's face. Eighteen. That's two years older than me.

"Your father was nuts about that little boy. He'd talk in funny voices and play silly games. He'd stay up late so I could sleep." Mom smiles slightly. "The baby gained weight. My mom started to accept things. The doctors said things were going well." Mom pauses and clears her throat.

"One night when the baby was six months old, I woke to hear your father yelling. I rushed to the crib. The baby was facedown, not breathing. Your dad tried mouth-to-mouth while I called the paramedics. They came right away, but they weren't able to save him. The baby was dead. SIDS. Sudden infant death syndrome. Nobody knows what causes it. Your dad felt terrible because he'd put the baby in the crib." Mom wipes tears from her eyes.

I feel sadness crushed by anger. "Why didn't you tell me?"

"We always meant to when you got older, but it got

harder, not easier." Mom looks straight ahead. "That wasn't right, but we didn't know how to talk about it. I think we felt guilty."

"Guilty about what?" That doesn't seem like a reason not to tell me.

"Guilty about getting pregnant. Guilty about the baby dying. Guilty about keeping it secret." Mom turns to me and her eyes are filled with tears. "I'm sorry."

I try to imagine Mom and Dad at that age. Dad getting Mom pregnant. Grandma and Drew angry at them. A difficult pregnancy. Premature birth. The baby dying. Their first baby. Is this why Dad keeps saying I've got plenty of time for that crap? Is this what he's afraid of?

I reach out to hug Mom. She holds on for a long time.

❚❚   ❚❚   ❚❚   That evening, Lucia meets me at her door. She's wearing a black turtleneck, and her hair is pulled back, showing more of her face. She looks beautiful.

"Come meet my mom." Lucia's perfume smells like spring.

In the living room, books fill the shelves and paintings cover the walls. One of them is of Lucia as a little girl. Lucia's mom is curled up on the couch in front of the fire.

"Mom, this is Miles."

"Hi, Miles." Lucia's mom gets up and shakes my hand. She has dark hair and big eyes like Lucia. She's wearing dangly hoop earrings.

"Pleased to meet you, Mrs. —"

"Call me Maggie."

"Okay." I don't usually call parents by their first name, but Lucia's mom seems different, more relaxed, like an adult who remembers what it's like to be a teenager.

"You two have fun. Lucia, I'd like you back by 11:00."

"How about 12:00?"

"I said 11:00." Lucia's mom points at her watch. Maybe she doesn't remember.

"That's too early. How about 11:30?"

"All right, 11:30 then. No later."

I'm amazed. Lucia's arguing for extra time — extra time to be with me.

▌▌ ▌▌ ▌▌ After the movie, we go to Juanita's, a little Mexican restaurant downtown. Lucia encourages me to order in Spanish, though I'm not very good.

"Un burrito con carne." The waitress smiles and waits patiently. "Un Coca-Cola."

Then Lucia orders and her Spanish flows. She and the waitress have a conversation, which gives me a chance

173

to stare. Lucia has nice nails with clear polish. I keep my bitten ones hidden beneath the table. She's got pretty eyebrows, too, not those thin things some girls think look good. And her eyes, I could look at them forever.

"What did you talk about?" I ask when the waitress leaves.

"She wanted to know why my boyfriend has black eyes."

"Really? What did you say?" Boyfriend. I like that.

"I told her you'd been getting into accidents."

"What else did you talk about?"

"Where she's from," Lucia says. "And she wanted to know where I lived in Mexico."

"You lived in Mexico?"

"Last year, I did a student exchange in Mérida."

"By yourself?"

"No, silly. I lived with the Aruellos, my host family, my Mexican family."

Lucia keeps surprising me. She's unlike anybody I know.

■■ ■■ ■■ Later we walk by the river. I've always liked living near it, but Lucia knows more about it after a few months than I do. She knows the Indian name Hahawakpa means "waterfall river" because of the falls farther east. She knows the history of fur trapping and French voyageurs trading with the Indians. She knows the names of different treaties and the dates they were broken. She knows about logging and the trees that were floated to Confluence to be milled into lumber. "That's why these big houses have all that wood trim," she says. "Lumber money."

She could be talking about anything and I'd listen. I love watching her hands fly as she talks. I'm so excited that I almost forget I've got two black eyes and a broken nose. And this afternoon Mom told me about a brother I never knew.

Lucia and I sit together on a bench that overlooks the river. The half moon shines through the trees. "Your turn," Lucia says. "Tell me about you."

I start talking. It's easier to tell Lucia things — big things — than anybody I've known. I tell her what Mom told me this afternoon, and she listens so intently that I keep going. "I wonder what it would've been like to have an older brother."

I tell her about Dad, how complicated he is. How he came up and pulled the hog ring out. How he saved me when the canoe hit the rock. "Mom says he loves me, but he won't say it. He constantly picks things apart and criticizes me. He's never satisfied."

I tell her about football. What a disaster it's been.

How we wanted to win State, but now can't win a game. How I wanted to be a star, but now don't play. How I lost my starting spot. "It hasn't been a total disaster, though, because I've gotten to know Sam. I've never played football with anybody like him."

"I know Sam from orchestra," Lucia says. "I'm glad you're friends."

I tell her about Zach. How we were best friends and did everything together. How he started shooting steroids with Tyson and wanted me to join. How he pulled away when I didn't. "That was hard, but it helped me figure out some stuff. Zach and I are different. He's totally into football. I used to be like that, but now there are other things I'm interested in."

"Like what?" Lucia asks.

"Like you." I look at her. She's such a good listener that I've been doing most of the talking. "What about you?"

Lucia starts slowly, then tells me about her parents' divorce when she was fourteen. "I can't imagine what they were thinking when they got married. They're completely different. Anyone can see that." She tells me about going back and forth between houses. "Usually it's okay, but sometimes I forget which stuff is where."

She tells me about her dad. "He's a human resources

director for a software company. He's got a new girlfriend and they're getting married next summer. They want me to be as excited as they are, but I'm not. She has a fifteen-year-old daughter, so I get a new stepsister, too. She's okay, but we're very different."

She tells me about her uncle Mario, who was killed in a car accident four years ago. "He was my favorite," she says. "I miss him."

"I'm sorry." I'm not sure what else to say. We stare out at the water together.

When we walk back along the river, we stop at the bridge and drop sticks. We run to the other side to see which one comes out first. Mine wins, so Lucia says two out of three, and then three out of five. She checks her watch and it's 11:20. We race back like we're running for the end zone.

"Thanks, Miles," she says at her house. "I had fun." Her face is flushed from the run.

"I did, too."

She kisses me on the cheek so fast I hardly realize what's happening. I don't have time to kiss her back.

But it still counts.

chapter twenty-nine

▐▌ ▐▌ ▐▌ "Yellow is the color of vomit. A puke color, a weak color. Blue and white are strong colors. They should beat yellow every time." Stahl's pacing back and forth in our locker room. "A win and we're in the play-offs. A loss and our season's over. It's that simple, men. We can beat these guys." Considering we've lost our last two and Lincoln is undefeated and ranked sixth in the state, this seems delusional.

"Remember, men, don't be intimidated," Stahl says. "Those guys put their pants on the same way you do — one leg at a time."

"Not quite," Sam whispers. I cover my mouth so Stahl won't see me laughing, but he's concentrating on the starters.

"Remember, men, there's no *I* in *team.*" Stahl writes it on the board.

"There isn't one in *dumb-ass* either," Sam says under his breath.

Even though it's a chilly night, lots of fans have come over from Lincoln. It's Parents' Night for us, and the stadium's packed. The Confluence pep band blasts out "Come Together," and Sam sings during hamstring stretches. He's the only guy who knows *all* the words to the song. "Geniuses, Beyond, geniuses, those lads from Liverpool. 'One thing I can tell you is you got to be free.' Fairly subversive song for Confluence, but absolutely perfect."

We switch to quad stretches and Sam keeps talking. "Got to soak it all in, Beyond. Last high school game for me. Never quite like this again."

Sam and I watch the panther mascot prowl the Lincoln sideline. "How about Panthers as a team name for Lincoln?"

"Hopeless," Sam says. "They don't have a single panther in town. They probably never have, unless some circus came through." He shakes his head at the mascot. "Pick a new one, *Miles.*"

I pause. "Navigators."

"Lincoln Navigators, that's better than Panthers." Sam nods. "Sponsorship possibilities, as well."

"Wait," I say. "I've got another one. Monument. The Lincoln Monument."

"Perfect. I love the strength, the singular nature of it. Lincoln Monument. That's solid, Beyond. You're showing signs of scrub leadership."

"How about Eagles, Sam? What do you think of Eagles for Confluence?"

"It's not bad. We've got lots of eagles because of the river. And the symbol fits the town."

"Proud, independent, all that."

"No, scavenger qualities."

"Eagles aren't scavengers."

"Yeah, they are. Eagles don't just glide around majestically. They eat roadkill and sit back and let ospreys fish and then swoop in and steal the catch. That fits fine as a symbol of Confluence."

How different the season has become. I used to focus on zone coverages and the opponents' tendencies. Now it's birds and team names.

Before the game, we line up facing the crowd for Parents' Night. Mom and Dad come onto the field and stand on either side of me. Mom wears my blue road jersey and Dad wears a Confluence sweatshirt.

"Number 42, Miles Manning, and his parents, Michael and Liz Manning." Mom beams at me and Dad looks at the ground. I check down the line to see Sam's folks. His dad's got a beard like Santa Claus and his mom is short and pretty. Sam waves to the crowd when he's announced.

After all the introductions, Mom hugs me. "I'm so proud of you, Miles. I love you."

I turn to Dad and he shakes my hand. "Have a good game," he says. What does that mean? I don't even play.

■ ■ ■ "Let's concentrate, men." Coach Stahl gathers us together. "This is the game of your life. It's what you were born to do. A victory over Lincoln would prove the experts wrong. Remember, just win, Eagles. Just win."

In the bleachers, Mom, Dad, and Martha look small in the crowd. I picture Dad as that young father giving mouth-to-mouth to his dead son. I don't even know the baby's name.

Lincoln's big and fast. Word spreads that college scouts are here to check out their running back, Number 44. On the first play, he hits Dawson, our linebacker, so hard that he gives him a concussion. On the next play, he smashes into Baker and knocks the wind out of him. When Baker staggers off, I hope for the call.

"Hedberg," Stahl shouts, and sends out another sophomore. I'm way better than Hedberg.

No score after the first quarter. The offense is doing nothing, but the defense has gotten a couple of breaks, a fumble recovery by Brooksy and another interception by Zach. Zach's having a great year — the kind of year I thought I'd have.

At halftime the score is 0–0 and Coach is pumped.

"Terrific first half, men. Lincoln came in here talking trash, acting like big shots, expecting a cakewalk. Now they realize it's a street fight. Men, you're giving 110 percent. Keep it up." Stahl claps his hands. "Remember, defense, if they don't score, they can't win. Offense, hold on to the ball. Keep blasting away. We've got 'em on their heels, men. Take it to 'em."

The crunch of helmets against shoulder pads carries across the field in the second half. Two more of our linebackers get hurt, and I'm stunned when Coach calls Sam's name.

"Hunter, get out there at middle linebacker and don't screw around."

Sam grabs his helmet and rushes onto the field. Last game of his senior year and he gets in. I'm thrilled for him, but envious, too.

On Sam's first play, they run up the middle. Sam stands up the blocker and collides with Number 44. Sam hangs on and wrestles him to the ground.

"Way to go, Gatherer." I knew he could play. Sam jumps up and hurries to the huddle.

With 2:14 left in the third quarter, the clock stops for an injury time-out. Brooksy is holding his ankle. He's been all over the field. Now he can barely walk. The trainers help him hobble to the bench.

Stahl calls Morriarty to replace him. Morriarty hasn't played much, and he'll have his hands full with 44. Immediately Lincoln runs the option, and Morriarty lunges for the quarterback, rather than staying with the tailback. The quarterback pitches and 44 runs fifteen yards before Zach pushes him out-of-bounds.

"Contain, Morriarty, contain," Stahl yells. "You've got the pitch. Don't get sucked in."

The next play Lincoln sweeps the other way. Our defense pursues. "Reverse," Stahl hollers as the wideout comes back. Morriarty's been caught inside, and the receiver has plenty of room. He gains twenty yards before Zach makes a touchdown-saving tackle.

"Morriarty, what are you doing? Get over here." Stahl throws off his headset. "Manning, get in for Morriarty at strong-side backer." I can't believe I heard right. I jump up from the bench. "Make sure you contain. You've got the pitch. You can do that, right?" Stahl slaps me on the helmet.

"Yes, Coach." I snap my chin strap and run onto the field. I'm thrilled to be out here but nervous about playing linebacker. I'm also worried about how hard 44 hits.

"Play it straight," Zach says in the huddle. He glances at me. "Five-three, cover three. Watch the pitch. Ready?"

"Break," we all shout. I'm back with the starters. I put my mouth guard in and tighten my gloves.

"Strong left," Zach shouts. Lincoln's huge. I set up outside the end. My job is to not let anyone get outside. Don't fall for the fake and then get burned on a pitch or a reverse.

"Hut one, hut two," the Lincoln quarterback calls. He takes the snap and runs at me. Number 44's behind him so I know it's an option. I stay wide with 44 and the quarterback pitches. I smash my shoulder into 44's legs and hang on as he falls down on my head. No gain.

My head's spinning from the hit as I untangle with 44. He's got a goatee that's familiar. I check his hand. T I M E on the right fingers holding on to the ball. The guy from Oxbow Lake. Next time, I'll hit him as hard as I can.

Quick pitch my way. I rush forward to contain. I turn to see something out of the side of my eye. *Bammm.* I'm leveled by the crackback. I lie on the ground struggling for breath. *Get up. Don't let them see you hurt.*

I stagger to Zach and jam my finger in his face. "Don't let me get blindsided. Give me a warning on the crackback."

Zach turns away. "Huddle up."

I gasp for breath in the huddle. "Four-three, cover two," Zach says. "Call out the crackbacks. Ready?"

"Break."

With four minutes left in the game, Sam strips the quarterback on a keeper.

"Fumble." The ball's in front of me. I dive and wrap my body around it. Offensive players grab and pull, but I hold on tight.

"Way to go, Man." Sam pulls me up.

"Great play, Gatherer." I slap him on the shoulder as we run off the field.

Three plays later, Monson breaks off tackle and hammers in for a score. We all go crazy. We're ahead of Lincoln. We haven't been ahead of anybody in three weeks. The band plays and the Confluence crowd keeps cheering. A group of girls sings and dances behind the bench.

"Say what?"

"That's the way we like it."

"Say what?"

"That's the way we like it."

"Say what?"

"That's the way, that's the way, that's the way we like it."

"Smash the Monument," I shout at Sam, who makes karate gestures.

"Get serious," Zach yells. He's right. We have to hold them again.

Sam, Zach, and I are playing the option on our side so well that Lincoln starts running the other way. This is the time when it's easy to slide too far. *Stay home*, I remind myself.

On second and six from our twenty-four, the Lincoln quarterback fakes left and drops back. Goatee's my responsibility, so I stick with him. The quarterback sets and throws. I close quickly and hammer Goatee while his arms are outstretched. He falls to the ground and the pass is incomplete.

"Payback!" I shout at him as teammates rush over. Goatee looks at me. I don't think he recognizes me. "Oxbow." I rub my nose.

It's third and three with 1:02 left in the game. Two more plays and we've pulled off the upset of the year.

"Strong left." I check the wideout as Lincoln lines up. His toes are turned in.

"Hut one." The quarterback pitches.

From the side, the wideout charges.

"Crackback," Zach hollers late, but it's better than nothing.

I pivot and hammer the receiver with a forearm to the head. I rush outside and meet Goatee one-on-one. He fakes inside, but I keep my eye on his waist the way Dad taught me. I lower my shoulder and smash him into the down marker. All the frustration of the past month is channeled into that hit.

"Time-out." He hops up. He's a tough guy.

"Final time-out, Lincoln," the referee calls.

Zach runs over to talk with Stahl.

"They've got to throw to the end zone here. How about a blitz?" Sam says.

"Smart call." I squirt water into my mouth and hand the bottle to Sam. I rinse my mouth and spit on the grass.

Zach runs back to the huddle. "Coach says four-three, cover one, straight up, no blitz. Line, get some pressure. Secondary, man-to-man. Play deep. Watch 44. Ready?"

"Break."

Lincoln lines up with Goatee on my side of the backfield. He's my guy on a pass.

"Hut one." Goatee swings out. He fakes in and cuts outside. I give him a cushion. The quarterback pump fakes, but I don't bite. Goatee breaks his pattern long. I bump him and run stride for stride down the sideline.

A roar rises from the Lincoln side of the field. I turn to see a receiver running into the end zone. Stahl smashes his clipboard to the ground. "Hedberg, how the hell could you let him get behind you?"

That's my old spot. If I'd been there, I wouldn't have gone for a pump fake to the other side of the field. I wouldn't have let him get behind me.

"Extra point, defense," Coach yells. "Manning, you're a safety."

As safety, I'm supposed to stay back and protect against the fake kick. Lincoln only needs the extra point to tie. I'm sure the way they drove down the field, they're confident they can win in overtime.

In the huddle, Zach says, "Let's get some penetration. Ready?"

"Break." As I walk to my end, I know Lincoln will kick. They won't risk losing the game on a fake. Why not gamble on the block to win? I grab Sam. "Can you take the guy on the end?"

"Sure."

Goatee lines up across from me. He looks like he's blocking all the way. So does everybody else. Sam slides over in front of Goatee and I move outside. I take a deep breath and visualize getting a hand on the ball.

"Hut one." Sam smashes into Goatee and I fly around the corner. Time slows and everything's clear. I dive at the spot in front of the kicker. The ball hits my arm. I got it. There's a scramble for the ball and Zach comes up with it.

Confluence fans explode with cheers. 0:00 on the clock. The referee blows his whistle. "We won. We won 7–6. We beat Lincoln." Teammates swarm, knock me to the grass, and pile on. I can barely breathe, but I don't care. We won. We won. We're going to the play-offs.

"Spectacular." Sam pulls me to my feet. "You're Miles Beyond."

"You're a star, Gatherer." I give him a bear hug. "We've got another game."

"Yeah, and I've got a date tonight with Julia, that hot cellist."

"Way to go."

Eagles fans of all shapes and sizes stream onto the field. People I don't know pound me on the pads. "Good game. Good game."

As we run off the field, I see Coach Sepolski standing with Halloran. Coach, who's lost weight, gives me a thumbs-up. I give him two back and run to see him.

"Way to go, Miles," he says. "Great players make great plays at crucial times."

"Thanks, Coach." We shake hands.

"Congratulations, Miles." Halloran slaps my back. "Beautiful block."

"Thanks, Mr. Halloran."

The celebration's in full swing in the locker room. Sam

jumps around taking his pants off two legs at a time. Jonesy and Stillwell laugh together by the trainer's room. I haven't seen them that happy since they were playing.

"One thing I can tell you is you got to be free," Sam hollers.

Jonesy slaps me on the shoulder. "Big-time play."

Even Zach comes over and says, "Good game, Man."

"Thanks." We bump fists.

Coach Stahl grabs me by the sleeve and pulls me into a corner. "Manning, what were you doing on that last play?"

"Going for the win, Coach. I thought they'd kick."

"It's not your job to think." Stahl's chomping his gum. "Your job is to be safety, to stay back in case there's a fake."

"But we won."

"That's not the point. The point is discipline, following directions, doing what you're told. And in all of those, you failed." Stahl spits out his gum. "You won't play another down for this team this year." He turns and walks away.

I'm too stunned to speak. I just got leveled by a crackback I never saw coming.

chapter thirty

▌▌ ▌▌ ▌▌ At Izzy's, people are celebrating. One guy runs around in his underwear screaming, "We're in the play-offs."

A group of girls sings loudly, "We are the Eagles, mighty, mighty Eagles. Everywhere we go, people want to know who we are, so we tell them. We are the Eagles, mighty, mighty Eagles."

I haven't told anyone what Stahl said. Maybe he'll change his mind. Stahl? Who am I kidding? There's no chance.

Zach's behind Tyson at the counter. They're getting burgers before going to a party at the Quarry. "You win on interceptions, Zach." I hand him his money.

"Hey, the season's not over."

"Yeah, but you're going to win."

"Thanks." He fans the five twenties and tucks them in his pocket. "We'll bet again next year."

"We'll see." Zach and I will always be connected by what we've done, but not in the same way. We've chosen different paths now.

At the back booth, I find Strangler and Jonesy.

"You're the star," Strangler says.

"Star, not Superstar." Jonesy points to himself.

Brooksy limps in on crutches with Megan. "Just a high-ankle sprain," he says. Megan leans his crutches against the wall and goes for food.

I can't keep quiet any longer. "Coach says I screwed up, that I was supposed to be safety on the extra point. He says I'm done playing this year."

Brooksy, Strangler, and Jonesy look stunned.

"You won the game," Strangler says.

"'Just win, Eagles. Just win.'" Brooksy imitates Stahl.

"That sucks." Jonesy shakes his head. "Something good finally happens, and Coach screws it up."

These guys are as angry as I am. I like hearing that. There's one other person I want to see. Lucia. She comes back from her dad's tomorrow. I wish she were here now.

❙❙   ❙❙   ❙❙   It's 1:20 when I get in, but Dad's still up. "Did you lock the door?"

"Yeah, it's locked."

"Are you sure?"

"Yes. What did you think of the game?"

"Good game." Dad sets down his *Sports Illustrated*.

"Coach was angry afterward. I had safety on the extra point, and instead I went for the block."

Dad doesn't say anything. He scrunches up his face.

"Well, that's a tough call. Sometimes you've got to take a chance and go for the win. Considering that offense of yours, that was a smart play."

I can't believe it's that simple when it comes. Dad gave me a compliment — a compliment about football. "Coach was angry. He said I wouldn't play again this year."

"That loser." Dad shakes his head. "You were one of his best players tonight."

"Thanks." I sit down on the couch.

"You can get that with young coaches," Dad says. "They're so insecure they focus more on being the boss than on winning."

I never thought of Stahl as being insecure. I thought he didn't like me. I'm surprised Dad's taking my side. "Dad, I talked with Mom."

"I know." He looks down.

"I'm sorry."

Dad doesn't respond and we sit without saying anything. Then I remember what I wanted to know. "What was his name?"

"Luke." Dad whispers it like a prayer.

"What was he like?"

"He was a good little guy. Dark hair, smiley." Dad's face softens. "Not a day goes by that I don't think of him."

It must have been so difficult. I try to picture Dad and Luke together.

"You know, when I was young, I always considered myself lucky," Dad says. "I was lucky in cards, lucky in sports, lucky in life. When Luke died, I never considered myself lucky again."

Dad pauses. "I was one room away and I didn't know what was happening. In my own house. I didn't do anything."

We sit in silence. Was losing Luke part of the reason Dad's been so hard on me? Did he see me as the replacement? Dad holds his hands together and spins his thumbs. His fingernails are short, like mine. He must bite his nails, too.

"Dad, where's Luke buried?"

"In the Veteran's Cemetery, by the airport in the Cities."

"Why there?"

"Your mother and I didn't have much money. We didn't know what to do. A friend said, 'You've been in the navy. You can have him buried at the Veteran's Cemetery.' I'm not sure about it now, though."

"Why?"

"No other family's there. The grave is one white marker among thousands."

"I'd like to see it."

"Yeah, we'll do that."

This isn't the type of conversation either of us is used to.

"Thanks, Dad."

"Yeah."

I know enough not to do something stupid like give him a hug.

■ ■ ■ Saturday morning when I call Drew, I recognize Stephen's voice.

"Hi, Stephen. It's Miles."

"Hey, Miles."

"How about those Patriots on Monday night?"

"Yeah. What a game. Drew and I were there. The place was going crazy," Stephen says. "I hear you guys had a big win last night, too."

"Yeah, we pulled off the upset."

"Congratulations. Here's Drew. He's dying to hear the details."

"Hi, Miles. You guys knocked off Lincoln." I'm surprised Drew's still following our games. "I've got it here. 'Miles Manning flew in to block the extra point for the Eagle victory.' You're the star, Miles."

"Not quite."

"What do you mean?"

"I was supposed to be safety on that play. Instead, I went for the block. Coach says he won't play me the rest of the year."

"But you made the play to win the game. That must count for something?"

"You'd think so." Talking about it won't change Stahl's decision, though. That's done. Then I remember why I called. "Drew, thank you."

"For what?"

"Mom and Dad told me about Luke."

"Ahhh." Drew pauses. "I'm glad, Miles."

"Me, too, but it takes some getting used to."

"Of course, but now you know. You've got something to work with."

"Yeah. Thanks, Drew."

"You're welcome, Miles. Say hi to everyone."

■ ■ ■ Out in the backyard, Martha and Mom drag pine branches to the bonfire. Dad collects brush all year and gets a burning permit in October. He throws the branches in and sparks fly. He loves watching things burn. "Nice of you to finally join us," he says.

I ignore it and haul some branches from the pile behind the garage.

"I just talked with Drew," I say. "He says hi to everyone."

"I like Drew," Martha says.

"How's he doing?" Mom takes off her gloves.

"Good," I say, though I forgot to ask. "He sounds good."

"How's Stephen?"

"He's good, too."

Dad pokes at the fire with a stick. He doesn't say anything. Sometimes that's a step forward. Sometimes not saying anything says plenty.

Martha and I go behind the garage for another load. We pull out dried cornstalks and squash vines. Hard to believe we got so much food from these dried-out plants.

"Mom and Dad told me about Luke." Martha looks up from yanking a vine.

"They told you together?"

"Yes, this morning. Dad said he and Mom wanted to talk to me. I knew it was important. They told me about Luke dying. Mom was crying. It's so sad, isn't it?"

"Yeah. I wonder what he'd be like." I try to imagine Luke now. He'd be two years older than me. "He'd be in college."

"He'd be the oldest," Martha says. "It helps to have an older brother."

I imagine shooting hoops with Luke. I imagine him protecting me. I'd have had somebody to talk to about Dad, somebody to help me figure him out.

Martha and I haul our load. Luke feels more like a brother, not just the baby who died.

At the fire, Dad wraps his arm around Mom's shoulder. Both their eyes are red.

"That's good," Dad says as Martha and I throw plants on the fire. They crackle and fizz and burst into flames.

▮▮ ▮▮ ▮▮ My favorite time of the year is the warm-up after the first frost. Some people call it Indian summer, but that doesn't make sense; Indians know their seasons. It's not as if they'd have a different summer.

Lucia and I walk along the west side of the river. A brown and black striped caterpillar creeps across the path.

"A woolly bear." Lucia bends down. "Feel it." She sets it in my hand.

It's not that soft. More bristly, like a brush. "When we were little, we thought you could predict how cold the winter would be by the woolly bear's coat."

"I still believe that," Lucia says.

"You do?"

"Yes. I like the idea that some animals know what's coming, that they can prepare."

I set the woolly bear on the other side of the path. Across the way, the Hahawakpa joins the Clearwater. The Hahawakpa is browner and stays separate from the Clearwater before they come together.

I tell Lucia about the game: getting to play with Sam, running into Goatee, blocking the kick, the joy of the victory. Then Stahl getting angry and telling me I won't play again this year.

"Wow," Lucia says.

"I'm glad I went for the block. I'd do it again. Even if Stahl says it's wrong."

"Yes." Lucia nods. "Yes."

I tell her about Dad saying I made a smart play and how much that means. I tell her how we all talked about Luke.

"Oh, Miles," she says.

As we walk north, the signs of people lessen. I think about next year. Who will be head coach, Sepolski or Stahl? Will Jonesy and Stillwell recover completely? How will Zach and I get along? Will things change with Dad?

"Look." Lucia stops. A fox and three kits bound in a meadow. They have gray backs and red ears and necks. The kits jump and tug at one another. They look like a cross between cats and dogs as they arch their backs and slink low to the ground.

"It's rare to see foxes in the middle of the day," Lucia says. "Aren't they beautiful?"

"Yeah, beautiful." *Like you,* I think as the foxes catch our scent and dart into the bushes.

"Let's take this path." Lucia chooses a gravel trail that changes to dirt, then to grass as it narrows to a single track. "It's a deer trail. I've seen them down here in the morning."

The path opens on to a clearing on the bank of the river. Grass has been matted down. On the opposite side, the burnt brown oak leaves — the last to go — flutter on branches. Gnawed trees and piles of wood chips show that beavers have been busy. I take off my sweatshirt and tie it around my waist.

One of the things I like about Lucia is how easy it is to be quiet with her. Some people have to talk all the time; she's not like that.

A creek trickles into the river, making its own small confluence. The river is lined with these. Some are large like the Hahawakpa. Most are small. Most don't even have names. All come together to form the river.

Lucia grabs my hand and points. A bald eagle glides above the water. I feel Lucia's warmth as we stand side by side. A dive, a stretch of claws, a snatch of fish.

"That's a good sign," Lucia says.

"Yes." Then I can't help myself. "Did you know, though, that eagles are major scavengers, that they eat roadkill and steal fish from ospreys?"

"Where did you hear that?" Lucia tilts her head back.

"I've been doing research. If I'm going to hang out with you, I've got to keep up on things."

Lucia laughs. "You're doing fine, Miles. Just fine."

I look into her eyes. They're clearer than the water, and deeper. Time slows like the present will last forever. This is exactly where I should be.

I lean forward and kiss Lucia.

Fine, just fine.

acknowledgments

Thanks to my teammates: Tim Bakken, Anamika Bhatnagar, Ian Byrne, Andrea Cascardi, James Coy, Mary Coy, Catherine Friend, John Kremer, David LaRochelle, Janet Lawson, Sophie Lenarz-Coy, Fiona McCrae, Patrick McCrae, John Moret, Jody Peterson-Lodge, Jon Quale, Colin Quinn, Cindy Rogers, Phyllis Root, Liz Szabla, Jane Resh Thomas, and the football players at Memorial High School.

Thanks to my coaches: Tom Partlow, Dick Tornowske, Phil Birkel, Ken Ripp, and Dave McGinnis.

Thanks to everyone at the Anderson Center for Interdisciplinary Studies for the gift of time and place.

Thanks to Tom Feelings for his remarkable book *The Middle Passage*.

And thanks to Dick Coy, Number 51, who taught me all he knew about football and emphasized that there was so much more.